D0837869

"If they run us off

Slade accelerated, hoping to outrun the pursuers, but the truck stayed close behind.

Another slam propelled them sideways.

Slade jerked the wheel, and his response had the car deviating through the ice-covered median as he battled the velocity forcing them out of control.

Heart jackhammering against his ribs, Slade pumped the brakes, but the car seemed to have a mind of its own and continued to speed up.

Asia screamed, and he jerked the wheel, avoiding a mile-marker pole by inches.

"I don't have brakes!" He slammed his foot repeatedly against the pedal, but it was useless.

"Slade, do something!"

But he couldn't stop.

Desperate, Slade yanked the wheel. The overcorrection sent the car careening into the ditch. "Hang on!"

They slammed on the driver's side, went airborne, then smashed down again. The impact shook every part of his body.

Each horrific recurring tug of gravity imprisoned them on a nightmare amusement park ride...

Sharee Stover is a Colorado native transplanted to Nebraska, where she lives with her husband, three children and two dogs. Her mother instilled in her the love of books before Sharee could read, along with the promise "If you can read, you can do anything." When she's not writing, she enjoys time with her family, long walks with her obnoxiously lovable German shepherd and crocheting. Find her at shareestover.com or on Twitter, @shareestover.

Books by Sharee Stover

Love Inspired Suspense

Secret Past
Silent Night Suspect

SILENT NIGHT SUSPECT

SHAREE STOVER

HARLEQUIN® LOVE INSPIRED® SUSPENSE

If you purchased this book without a cover you should be aware that this book is stolen property. It was reported as "unsold and destroyed" to the publisher, and neither the author nor the publisher has received any payment for this "stripped book."

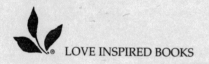 LOVE INSPIRED BOOKS

Recycling programs for this product may not exist in your area.

ISBN-13: 978-1-335-23253-3

Silent Night Suspect

Copyright © 2019 by Sharee Stover

All rights reserved. Except for use in any review, the reproduction or utilization of this work in whole or in part in any form by any electronic, mechanical or other means, now known or hereafter invented, including xerography, photocopying and recording, or in any information storage or retrieval system, is forbidden without the written permission of the editorial office, Love Inspired Books, 195 Broadway, New York, NY 10007 U.S.A.

This is a work of fiction. Names, characters, places and incidents are either the product of the author's imagination or are used fictitiously, and any resemblance to actual persons, living or dead, business establishments, events or locales is entirely coincidental.

This edition published by arrangement with Love Inspired Books.

® and TM are trademarks of Love Inspired Books, used under license. Trademarks indicated with ® are registered in the United States Patent and Trademark Office, the Canadian Intellectual Property Office and in other countries.

www.Harlequin.com

Printed in U.S.A.

What time I am afraid, I will trust in thee.
–*Psalm* 56:3

To my Lord and Savior, Jesus. All glory and honor belong to You. And for Jim, Tawny, Cody and Andi because you see the best in me, even when I can't.

Acknowledgments

I've heard it said it takes a village to raise a child, and I think that's applicable to writing a book, as well. I am beyond grateful for the incredible group of people who support and encourage me through every sentence.

Many thanks to:

My editor, Emily Rodmell, for sticking with me as this story evolved and for your wisdom in its development.

Tina Radcliffe for seeing past the dry bones and helping me to revive and breathe life back into this book.

Connie, Jackie, Rhonda, Sherrinda and all of the Writing Sisters. You all are precious.

ONE

Asia Stratton's gaze remained transfixed on the lifeless eyes staring back at her. Dark pools—so black they appeared to be bottomless holes—silently demanded an explanation for the single bullet wound to the center of the man's forehead.

An explanation she couldn't provide.

"Asia, drop the gun. Put your hands up," a male voice ordered.

She jerked at the mention of her name and squinted against the blinding light veiling the stranger in the doorway. Darkness had fallen, and Nebraska's icy winter wind blasted through the unfamiliar living room.

The dead man's silent inquisition beckoned, and Asia reverted her attention to him.

"I said, drop the gun," the intruder repeated.

His words trickled through the fog in her brain and she gasped at the Glock gripped in her palm. Asia released her hold, and the weapon toppled from her shaking hands onto the dirty carpet. She lifted her arms in obedience, sending a jolt of pain radiating up her shoulder. She cried out, then caught sight of the crimson stain marring her white blouse.

"Keep your hands up! Don't make any sudden moves." In her peripheral, she saw the man enter, taking cautious, steady steps, gun trained on her. His familiar uniform publicized his law enforcement authority. "Don't move," he repeated, then kicked the door closed behind him, sending another wave of cold air her way.

She winced and shivered, keeping her arms raised as high as she could tolerate. The flickering glow from the muted television, combined with the officer's flashlight beam bouncing off the walls, rivaled the intense headache pounding in Asia's skull. Dizziness swirled, and nausea overwhelmed her senses.

The trooper stepped between her and the dead stranger opposite her. "Whose blood is on your blouse? Yours or his?" He turned off the flashlight, then used it to gesture at her.

Asia swallowed. "Mine. I think?"

"Lower your hands slowly, keeping them where I can see them."

Her gaze traveled up the barrel of the officer's gun until she focused on his face. Fear morphed into confusion, only to be replaced by annoyance. Of all the cops in the world, it had to be *him*. Nebraska state trooper Slade Jackson. Her deceased husband's ex-partner—and her backstabbing former high school boyfriend.

"Very slowly, extend your hands toward me."

An argument lingered on her lips, but the murkiness in her brain had her complying. She momentarily broke her gaze from the dead man. "I don't—"

Slade encircled her wrists with cold metal, startling her. "This is necessary for your safety and mine. Protocol." The click of handcuffs stabbed her with irritation. "I'm supposed to secure your arms behind your back, but with your shoulder injury…"

He was justifying handcuffing her? She stared at him,

hoping to mask her fear. "Are you kidding me? Handcuffs? You've known me since kindergarten."

Her words had no effect on him. Of course not. Slade was always the rule follower. Procedure Boy. Even when it meant destroying other people's lives.

Slade stepped to her side and kicked the Glock out of reach. "Is there anyone else here?" His gaze bounced between Asia and the small hallway behind her. The questions etched on his face no doubt mirrored her own bewilderment.

"I don't... I didn't..." She gulped, trying to form an intelligent sentence. How could she answer him when she had no answers? She surveyed the unfamiliar compact living room. Where was she, and how had she gotten here?

He pressed a cloth against her shoulder. "It'll be a little tough with the handcuffs but keep pressure on the wound."

She held the fabric against her chest, which tightened with each breath.

He knelt and pushed his fingers against the deceased's neck. Asia rolled her eyes. Surely he needed to check off a rules-for-finding-a-dead-body box somewhere.

"Why are you here with Nevil Quenten?" Wide-eyed, Slade spoke in a hushed tone and pointed at the dead guy.

"*That's* Nevil Quenten? The Colombian drug cartel leader?" Asia squeaked, her gaze ricocheting between Slade and the man. "Zander talked about him, but somehow I envisioned him...more evil looking."

"Sorry to disappoint you, but this is Quenten." Slade held his service weapon in one hand and offered to help her stand with the other. He tilted his head as if to say *trust me*.

No way. She gave the proffered hand a cursory glance as she shifted. The pin-prickling sensation made her yelp. "My legs are asleep. Give me a second."

He stepped back, granting her space, but never lowered

his weapon. Asia attempted to get to her feet again, surrendering to Slade's outstretched palm as he pulled her upright. At five feet ten inches, she stood nose to nose with Slade. The quick change of position had her teetering off balance on her tingling legs. His steadying contact stabilized her. Grounded her. Like he'd done when they were kids.

Slade remained silent, helping her to the closest of the three green-and-white lawn chairs that passed for living room furniture.

She paused.

"Don't be difficult," he cautioned.

Asia bristled against his touch and shifted away from his hold with a huff. "I'm not being difficult. For your information, I'm worried the chair might fall apart." She nodded at the frayed material.

"It'll be fine," he assured her.

She frowned and dropped onto the seat without comment, hoping the fabric would rip and prove him wrong.

"Stay put."

"You're leaving me alone? With him?" She shivered and shrank back, as if the dead man would rise and attack her.

"He's not going anywhere. Just wait here." Slade pressed down on her uninjured shoulder, emphasizing the instructions before moving into the hallway.

Asia studied Nevil Quenten, torn between terror and curiosity. The man's tidy appearance complete with a gray suit and navy tie reminded her of a bank manager. But he was an unmerciful drug cartel leader who had destroyed her deceased husband, Zander.

And now Nevil Quenten was dead. In the same room as her.

She shifted farther to the side and racked her brain. The dissipating haze brought no great revelations. Why couldn't she remember anything? The abyss in her mind explained nothing about her present conditions, and the strain exaggerated the headache clawing its way across her temples.

She scanned the foreign space with its worn brown carpet and plastic walls. Not drywall? What kind of house had plastic walls? A mobile, trailer or prefabricated home? She had no friends or acquaintances who lived in any houses like those. *Why can't I remember anything?*

The rancid scent of urine and rotting food added to her queasiness. Lawn chairs half circled the dated nineteen-inch television. Empty blue-and-white pizza boxes stacked in a haphazard tower decorated the floor beside the yellow refrigerator in the tiny kitchenette to her left. A pathetic string of silver garland hung from the broken window blinds in uneven loops, and chipped red Christmas ornaments tugged the tinsel downward. The display provided a sad attempt at sprucing the place up with holiday spirit.

Where was she? Anxiety ratcheted, twisting her stomach into knots.

Slade returned and slipped his service weapon into the holster. "The house is clear."

"What about the outside?"

He quirked an eyebrow, annoyance tainting his tone. "I checked the perimeter before entering this place. It's protocol." He crossed his arms over his chest. "Why did you text me to meet you here? To show me you killed him?"

That got her attention. "I didn't kill anyone, and I never sent you a text! I have no idea what you're talking about." She might not be able to explain how she'd gotten here, but murder wasn't in her DNA. And texting her ex-boyfriend ranked among the top five on her not-in-this-lifetime list.

He walked toward the kitchenette and flipped on the switch, illuminating the space. She regarded his solid build outlined in the starched navy blue uniform with Ginsu-knife creases. Not a dark hair out of place in his meticulous, close-cropped style. Zander had been the perfect state trooper too. Might've still been if he'd gotten the help he needed before—

"What's going on here?" Slade probed, facing her in the classic feet-shoulder-width-apart power stance.

Asia contemplated her answer. They'd written the Miranda warning for occasions such as this, but that applied to real criminals. *You have the right to remain silent…*starting now. She had nothing to hide, since she had no memory of whatever she should be hiding, anyway.

"I came to just before you walked in. I have no idea how long I was unconscious, and your knock on the door jarred me into this bizarre scene. I don't remember anything beyond being in my apartment getting ready for bed."

Slade's frown conveyed his skepticism.

"You wanted the truth and I'm telling you," Asia continued, her words tumbling out faster. "When I caught sight of the *dead guy*—" She tried to point to Nevil's body, but the handcuffs restricted her movement and the bloodied cloth tumbled to the floor. "I reacted. Just grabbed the thing off my lap and then you walked in." She nodded toward the Glock. "I didn't even realize it was a gun."

"You don't seriously expect me to believe that." Slade stooped, lifted the cloth and reapplied it to her shoulder before moving to the TV and shutting it off. Silence hovered between them like an invisible shield of disbelief. "I need you to tell me what happened before I got here. I can't hold off calling this in to dispatch any longer." His caramel-brown eyes pleaded with her to respond, though he remained in his defensive posture.

Their history should eliminate the caution he maintained. They'd grown up together, had dated through most of high school, had basically known each other forever. Surely those memories counted for something. Asia's gaze jerked from Slade to Nevil's body, then to the weapon on the floor. *Please, Lord, make my memory return. Give me wisdom in what to say.*

"Was it self-defense?"

She met Slade's penetrating look. All they were missing was a spotlight and metal table for the way his interrogation was going. "Nice try, but I didn't kill him."

"I saw you holding the gun."

The allegation stung, raising her defenses. "Are you listening at all? I told you, I went to bed early. In my apartment. Next thing I know, I'm waking up here. Wherever 'here' is."

"Can anyone corroborate your story?"

Asia sat up straighter and lifted her chin. "No, because I was alone. And it's not a story. It's the truth."

"Fine. If you refuse to cooperate, we'll stick to procedures and I'll treat you like any other murder suspect." Slade depressed the button on his portable shoulder mic. "Request assistance and ambulance. One injured suspect, one dead, possibly more people unknown and unaccounted for."

"Ten-four, twenty-two fifty," the dispatcher confirmed.

Asia jumped to her feet, unable to breathe past the vise squeezing her chest. Ten fifty at night. How long had she been here? "What day is it?"

Slade tilted his head. "Don't even try the helpless damsel thing."

She clamped a hand onto his forearm clumsily and demanded, "Tell me what day it is."

He plucked away her fingers then led her back to the chair. "You have to sit down. We don't need you losing more blood."

"The date?" Asia insisted, searching his eyes.

He cocked his head to the side and blew out a breath. "December twenty-second."

"Are you sure?" The room swayed, and Asia's hands fell heavy in her lap.

"Of course I'm sure." Slade adjusted his mic wire, clearly frustrated. Well, he wasn't the only one.

"No. That's not possible," Asia mumbled. "It can't be." Her thoughts traveled to her color-coded salon appointment book. Pink for haircuts, blue for pedicures—and December twentieth in bold print at the top of the page. Horrified, she doubled over, pressing her bound wrists against her stomach.

"Hey, are you okay?" The warmth of Slade's hand on her shoulder kept her fixed in the moment, though she longed to escape.

"I don't... How can it be December twenty-second?" She sat up. "How did I lose two days of my life?"

He shook his head. "Asia, stop messing around. I've gotta start this report before backup arrives."

She blasted him with her best death glare. "Slade, I'd love to spout the answers you want, but let me clue you in. I was in my apartment on December twentieth. It was payday, and I was trying to figure out how to make my rent. One of the many joys of being a widow whose drug-addicted husband took everything and sold it to supply his habit."

Doubt marked his frown, and he knelt beside the Glock, surveying but not touching the weapon. "Still doesn't explain why you were pointing a gun at Quenten."

Asia bit her lip, scanning the room again, and landed on Slade's unbelieving frown. "I'm trying to help you, but you can see how this will sound to the district attorney."

She stiffened. "I *am* being honest, and no, thanks—I've seen your idea of help."

The verbal slap tightened Slade's jaw and irritation flashed in his eyes, but his tone remained unwavering. "Asia, I'll never be able to tell you how sorry I am that Zander is gone. There's not a day that goes by that I don't think about him. He was my friend, my partner."

"Wow, beautiful. Is that the same little speech you told Sergeant Oliver before you betrayed Zander?" She pinned him with a glower. Slade was a traitor, and he'd destroyed her life.

They held their wordless staredown until Slade glanced out the window, watching for backup. "Zander made his own choices and put us both in an impossible situation, including backing me against the wall. Turning him in was my duty. I had no other options." He spun to face her.

Asia looked away. Choices. There was no disputing the facts. Zander had chosen drugs, a plethora of other women and repeated binges. The combination proved to be the catalyst for their separation a year before his death had made her a widow at thirty-four. He'd walked a dangerous path, leading a double life as a trooper and working for Quenten. Eventually, it was bound to catch up to him. Asia had warned him repeatedly to get help and talk to Sergeant Oliver. In the end, Zander's murder hadn't been a surprise. He'd played too long with a dangerous, consuming fire.

Still, Asia would never pretend to be okay with Slade's method of handling things. He could've helped Zander. Been a real friend. Instead, Slade earned accolades by arresting Zander and putting a homing target on him that led Quenten's men right to him. They'd silenced Zander permanently as a result of Slade's by-the-book philosophy.

Asia had lost everything. And Zander was dead.

Slade was to blame. It was that simple.

The familiar sorrow she'd befriended beckoned again. Slade exhaled, and his posture relaxed. "What happened with Quenten?" A gentle tone slipped through, reminding her of the boy she'd once known. He withdrew a small notepad from his uniform pocket.

Stay angry. It's safer. Easier. "If you ask me a hundred more times, I will tell you the same thing. I don't know how or why I'm here. I never shot him. And I. Don't. Remember. Anything." Asia kept her voice tight and controlled, maintaining her composure to prevent any weakness from leaking through.

"If you have no memories of being here, how can you be sure you didn't shoot Quenten?"

Asia forced her cuffed, shaking hands flat against her thighs. "My turn to ask questions. How's your new position with the drug task force? Tell me, Slade—did your promotion come as a reward for betraying your partner? Or was it a consolation prize for arresting him and giving his murderer easy access to kill Zander?"

Slade flinched at the verbal attack. Deserved, but painful nonetheless. The venomous words stabbed his heart, a vicious reminder of his failures. His guilt. And he couldn't agree with Asia more.

She'd never forgive him. And she'd never understand that turning in Zander had been the hardest thing he'd ever done. Maybe to some degree, she was right to blame him for Zander's death. But he hadn't complied with Zander's unfathomable request to arrest him for the pleasure of earning a promotion, or anything else self-serving.

Zander's plan should've been simple. Slade would publicly arrest him so Quenten would believe his insider had been compromised. Then Zander would compile whatever evidence he'd assured Slade he had, ferret out the mole within the Nebraska State Patrol, turn state's evidence and go into WITSEC. Zander had refused to share the details with Slade, wanting to protect him by not dragging him into the mire.

Except everything went horribly wrong, and within twenty-four hours of being arrested, processed and released on bail, Zander was murdered. Slade had no evidence of corruption, no proof of a mole, and he'd been marked a backstabbing cop for turning in his partner. He bore Asia's blame and anger and was left in an impossible situation of keeping Zander's secret even after his death.

"A good partner would've helped him instead of taking the first opportunity to prove your disloyalty for a lousy promotion."

Slade didn't refute her words, but if she only knew the truth… Zander always got everything he wanted, including Asia. Slade had respected her decision all those years ago, tucking his own feelings far away where they couldn't hurt either of them. He inhaled and replied with stale facts. "He was a drug-addicted thief working with that guy." He pointed at Quenten's body. "Which brings me back to what you're doing here with a gun and a dead man. The circumstances, such as they are, aren't looking good for you."

"I'm fully aware of how this looks. Contrary to yours and the entire state patrol's beliefs, I'm not stupid."

His radio squawked, halting their conversation.

"Go ahead," he answered.

"Multivehicle injury accident with confirmed fatality on Highway 275. Backup is delayed. Will dispatch next closest ambulance," the dispatcher rattled on.

Just another night in rural Nebraska. Never enough responders, and everything happened at once. "Ten-four," he acknowledged. "Guess it'll be a bit before they get here. So how about if we start over? First, your injury appears to be a through-and-through gunshot wound, from the little I can see. May I take a closer look?"

She glanced down and removed the cloth. "Fine."

Slade examined her bleeding shoulder then pressed the fabric tighter against the injury. "Yep, looks like the bullet went clean through." A blood-matted section on the back of her head caught his eye. "You've got a head injury too."

"What?"

When he reached out to examine her, she flinched at his touch. He retracted his hand, the sting of her rejection piercing his heart. They used to be friends. "I won't hurt you." *I've done enough damage already to last a lifetime.* "I only want to check the injury."

"Okay."

He withdrew his flashlight, then separated her raven shoulder-length hair clotted with dried blood to reveal a goose egg.

"Ouch!" Asia dodged to the side.

He jerked back his hand and replaced the light in his gun belt. "Sorry. Any idea where you got that knot?"

"No."

"Do you have any other injuries?"

She narrowed her eyes. "If I weren't handcuffed, I might be able to answer your question."

The department-issued restraints latched on her wrists tore at him. Never in his wildest imagination had he considered the possibility of arresting Asia. "It's protocol."

"Right—I forgot you never break the rules." Her uncharacteristic sarcasm sliced through his heart.

When had she grown so cold toward him? The sweet girl he'd known all his life had morphed into an angry woman, but he saw fear in her dark eyes masked behind the facade of her bitter tone.

"I'll remove the handcuffs, but don't try anything stupid."

"You're joking, right?"

Joking was the furthest thing from his mind. This whole situation was beyond his comprehension. He knelt in front of her and removed the cuffs. Asia was the last person he'd thought capable of murder. Almost fifteen years in law enforcement had awakened him to a lot of unbelievable realities. Still, his gut said she wasn't guilty. Or was it his heart?

Asia lifted her hand and rubbed her wrists, then gingerly fingered the head wound and winced. "That solves the mystery behind my headache and the internal bullhorn amplifying every word you speak."

Slade stilled her with a raised palm. It was too quiet.

"I—"

"Shh."

She glared at him but remained silent.

He stepped into the hallway and scanned the two bedrooms again. He entered the back bedroom, stepping around the king-size mattress and knee-high junk piles to the window. Slade peered out of the broken blinds into the darkness.

The trailer was located in the middle of an abandoned farm away from the road. A large dilapidated shed surrounded by mounds of jalopy cars sat two hundred feet from the mobile and close to the neglected cornfields. Slade lifted the window and scanned the area with his flashlight, illuminating the ominous shadows.

Nothing but the wind whipping over the land and trees greeted him. He slid the window closed and repeated his surveillance in the bedroom facing the front of the property. Trash bags and boxes stacked high obscured the window, forcing Slade to move around the mess. He shifted between the towering displays of clutter and glanced out the dirty glass. A glimmering light flickered in the distance.

A shiver writhed up his spine. The light faded. A passing car on the county road?

He returned to the small living room. The home had to

be at least thirty years old. Deserted and in the middle of nowhere. Not a place he'd expect to find Asia. So why had she texted him to meet her here?

A sense of foreboding hung heavy in the air like the putrid atmosphere. Maybe he should just arrest her and get out of here. The isolated locale left them exposed and too far from help. Whatever her situation, they'd work out the details at the patrol office. He closed the space between them, determined. "I think we'd better—"

Headlights beamed through the window and the crunching of tires on the ice-covered snow drew Slade's attention. A large black vehicle sped toward the house. Too fast. "Get down!" He tugged Asia to the floor.

Slade crouched and peered through the bottom corner of the blinds. A barrage of gunshots turned his patrol car into Swiss cheese.

"Shots fired! Shots fired! Newer-model black SUV. Need backup! Now!" His voice reverberated and increased an octave, hollow in his own ears. Anticipating a blast, he shielded Asia with his body.

Several seconds passed with no explosion. Pulse drumming and fury radiating up his neck, Slade shifted to get another glance outside. "Stay down." His hands shook with adrenaline as he pushed the blinds aside.

The assailants circled on the snow-covered ground, filtering headlights inside again. They were coming back! He dived, covering Asia a second time.

Bullets blasted through the home, shattering the window and raining glass.

The dispatcher's robotic response melded into the background of machine gun fire. Slade tucked Asia under him, protecting her from the debris pelting his neck and arms.

"We've got to get out of here." He glanced up, catching sight of the hallway. Grateful he'd cleared the property earlier, he considered their only exit strategy. The bathroom and bedroom at the front of the home would shield them until they climbed out the rear-facing bedroom window.

Rhythmic pinging penetrated the fabricated home's thin walls, and the TV took several hits before emitting sparks.

"Stay low and move to the back."

"Okay," she cried over the noise.

They army-crawled through the hallway and into the bedroom. Slade pushed the door shut, providing a barrier—albeit a flimsy one—against the firepower.

"Can you climb out the window?" He lifted the latch, pulled open the tall rectangular glass and shoved out the screen. "It's only a few feet down. I'll lower you."

"I've got it." Asia moved in front of him and scrambled through. She perched on the ledge before hopping down.

Slade followed behind and grasped her arm. "Hold on."

The gunfire ceased, leaving an eerie calm hanging in the air.

Had the shooters gone?

The ground was covered in hard-packed snow and their footprints would be easily visible. Only two viable options of escape remained. Run through the cornfields and hope they reached help before the men found them or hide in the shed. If they ran to the front of the house and the men were waiting, they were dead. Scattered assorted metal junk pieces covered the backyard. They'd have to use the debris in a disorganized game of hopscotch to hide their location. Asia's compromised state and blood loss combined with his undrivable unit meant hiding was the only logical choice. They'd have to take their chances.

"Follow me and step only on the junk. Do not let your feet hit the snow." Slade gripped Asia's hand and they made their way to the random assortment of hubcaps, cinder blocks and other unidentifiable scraps.

They neared the shed and Slade peered over his shoulder. Men's voices echoed inside the house. They'd pursue as soon as they spied the open window.

He shoved aside the shed's rusted metal door hanging by one rotted hinge.

"Is this safe?" Asia whispered, squeezing through the gap.

It was a good question. "Get behind the hood." Slade gestured toward an old truck hood leaning against a dried and decaying bale of straw.

Asia maneuvered around the junk and squatted. Slade joined her and inspected the shadowy space. His flashlight would prove beneficial, but advertising their location would be unwise. Darkness hid things he'd rather not spot, anyway. Various vehicle parts including two more hoods pressed against the far wall, shielding them on all sides. A barricade of automotive leftovers. *Please, Lord, let them protect us.*

"Don't make a sound," he whispered, silencing his radio.

Together they faced the door. A sliver of an opening provided a decent vantage point of the back of the home but trapped them with no other way out.

"They escaped." A man's voice carried from the house across the open land.

"They found the window," Slade murmured, more to himself than Asia. "Stay behind me," he warned, moving in front of her.

"Hey, I need—"

"Not now," he hissed. Weapon poised, Slade peered around the oxidized hood and spoke into his shoulder mic. "Shooters still on the premises." The speaker remained muted because it didn't matter what the dispatcher said. They had to get out of here—and fast.

Where was his backup? Slade angled past the bales and

crept toward the entrance. Asia started to follow, but he halted her with his hand. He peeked through the crack between the door and the frame. Figures moved inside the bedroom. How many were there?

"At least Nevil Quenten is dead." The man's booming voice made him easy to distinguish.

"Excellent," the first replied. "Where're the cop and woman?"

Slade stiffened. What had Asia gotten herself into?

"They got away. You need shooting lessons. All that damage and you still didn't kill them."

Asia shifted behind him and a hollow ting resounded in the small shed. Slade jerked as the offending noisemaker rolled to his feet. A hubcap.

"Quiet! I heard something," the voice outside demanded.

Slade moved to where Asia stood near the hood and bales. He pinned her with a glare. She shrugged and mouthed "Sorry." Tugging her down, he crouched with her behind the metal barrier. He strained to hear the men's conversation.

"There's nothing out there. I told you, they escaped," the other argued.

"No. I see a shed. That's where they are."

Within seconds, the crunching of boots on snow drew closer.

Slade surveyed the confined space again, searching for a way out. They were trapped.

The steps paused outside the shed.

Please, God, get backup here. Fast!

"Knock, knock." The man's taunts were followed by two quick raps on the door.

Slade held his breath, gun at the ready and heart drumming in his ears. He might be able to outshoot them, but were there more intruders in the vehicle? If he missed, and Asia was hit… No, he'd have to be dead on target.

A rat skittered over Slade's boot, and he flinched, nearly squeezing the trigger. The rodent scurried out of the opening, evoking a curse from the intruder.

"Aw, what's the matter? Scared of the dark or the little mouse?" The second man roared with laughter. His voice echoed, confirming he was farther away.

"It's not funny. Rats carry disease," the first whined.

Footsteps drew closer. "Move, so I can look inside."

"Forget it. I'll take care of them from here."

Slade interpreted the warning and shoved Asia to the cement floor, covering her with his body. Bullets pinged all around them in rapid succession. The hood and the bale suffered the brunt of the attack, spitting shards of straw like confetti at a parade.

At last, the rain of fire stopped. Asia's staccato panting lingered, but to her credit, she never uttered a sound.

Slade lifted his head and pressed his fingers against his lips, reminding Asia to keep quiet. She nodded. Slade shifted into a crouch while considering the number of bullets in his magazine. Were there enough for him to blast their way free of the shed?

"Let's see if you win the prize." The door creaked, and the intruder's hand grasped the metal.

Slade aimed, prepared to fire. He'd have to take his chances and pray he hit his target the first time.

And then he paused at the beautiful scream of sirens in the distance.

TWO

"One of those blue-and-red-flashing beasts better be an ambulance," Slade murmured.

Sound carried over miles in the flatlands of Nebraska. Only a few minutes had passed since the men had fled at the wail of the approaching emergency vehicles. Each rendition acted like a tornado siren, warning time was running out to get Asia talking.

Slade knelt beside her. The uneven rotting boards of the pockmarked trailer's porch steps dug into his knees, and the cold pierced through his long-sleeved uniform shirt. At least Asia hadn't balked at wearing his patrol-issued coat. He'd draped it over her shoulders and kept his hand on her back to maintain pressure against the bullet's exit wound. Concern flowed through him at the soaked material. She was losing blood at an excessive rate, and his internal frustration boiled over at her silence.

Asia leaned against the paint-chipped railing, applying another gauze compress to the front of her shoulder. She'd given his mumbled declaration a second-long glance but had remained mute.

He sat and made one final plea to her stubborn denial. "I want to help you."

"I know." She shifted and met his gaze with a softened

expression. "The cavalry is almost here. You'd better put on the handcuffs." Asia held out her wrists, wincing with the movement.

"Don't worry about them. Focus on staying awake and keeping pressure on the wound." Slade gently returned her hand over the injury, noting the smoothness of her skin. His attention shifted to the dark red stain mixed with streaks of grease and dirt marring her white blouse. The grime did nothing to distract from her beauty. Her shoulder-length hair hung in disheveled, shadowy rivers, framing her oval face and dark eyes.

"I'm fine," she rasped.

"You've always been a terrible actor."

The corners of Asia's lips tugged upward, then fell away as her eyes fluttered closed.

"No sleeping for you," he prodded. If she had a concussion, she had to stay awake.

"I'm fine," Asia repeated, righting herself and backing from his touch. Her shoulders slumped and seemed to bear the weight of the world.

Slade concentrated on the flashing lights, fighting the desire to remove her burdens. *She couldn't be guilty.* The internal policy and procedure manual played like background music in his brain, battling with concern for her well-being. "Do you remember anything else?"

Dumb question since he'd already asked her the same thing a hundred different ways, but he had to help her. He owed it to Zander—and to Asia. "Maybe you recall being attacked? Or waking in a trunk?"

The briefest hint of a smile broke through her downcast expression. "You watch too many television shows." She shook her head, then glanced down. "You're doing your job, and I need to follow the rules. I won't fight."

Rumbling engines barreled down the snow-packed gravel

driveway. Slade recognized his sergeant's patrol car—the twin of his own pre-bullet-ridden vehicle—leading the pack with Slade's brother Trooper Trey Jackson's white K9 pickup following closely behind. Two brown sedans with sheriff county logos and an ambulance joined the entourage.

"Are you able to walk?" Slade offered his hand. "Otherwise, I'll carry you to the ambulance."

Asia straightened as if he'd cattle prodded her. "You're not carrying me anywhere." She grasped hold of the railing and pulled herself up. Her obstinacy rivaled any mule.

Slade started to touch the small of her back, then thought better of it. "Just stay by my side and let me do the talking." For once, she didn't argue, and they walked toward Sergeant Oliver's vehicle.

"Jackson! What's going on?" Oliver yelled, clambering out of the attractive low-profile Charger. The twenty-pound gun belt, Kevlar vest and the man's bulky stature made for a difficult exit from the car. "Are you all right?" His gaze bounced from Slade to Asia, registering her presence. "Mrs. Stratton?" Oliver's confusion said he too was trying to make sense of the situation.

"Shooters bolted when they heard the sirens." Slade stepped protectively closer to Asia's side.

"What happened to your car?" Oliver asked, mouth agape.

The newer vehicle's damage costs would make their way up the chain of command and right to the colonel's desk. After Slade spent the next week filling out paperwork.

Two EMTs advanced, and Slade sent a silent prayer of thanks for the interruption. "Let me get Asia—Mrs. Stratton—taken care of." He excused himself from Oliver and addressed the medics. They visually assessed her condition as Slade provided a robotic report. "Mrs. Stratton has a bullet wound to her shoulder—appears to be a through and through—and she has a contusion on the back of her head."

The shorter of the two men nodded vehemently while charting on his iPad. White embroidery on his blue uniform shirt spelled Hereford. Easy to remember. Uncle Irwin had bred Hereford cows. The man's youthful appearance had Slade questioning whether he was even old enough to drive the rig. Then he realized he sounded like his father, always complaining that everyone else was getting younger when the reality was he was the one aging.

"I'll get the stretcher." The taller EMT jogged to the ambulance before Slade caught sight of his name on his badge.

"I'm not riding on a stretcher." Asia shook her head, one palm up in defense.

"Ma'am," Hereford began.

"I'll assist her to the rig," Slade promised, not wanting her to become more agitated. What was wrong with her?

Hereford frowned and joined his partner.

Slade moved between Asia and the EMTs as a high school memory bounced to the forefront of his mind. "Still claustrophobic? Or are you boycotting ambulances?" he teased, hoping to lighten her anxiety.

She blinked, and understanding shone in her eyes. "You remember?"

"Um, yeah. You nearly capsized our canoe in the amusement park's tunnel of love." His neck warmed at the romantic recollection of their junior year in high school. He'd spent half his earnings from the grain elevator just to win Asia a giant teddy bear. That had been a wonderful time.

Slade shoved the painful reminder down. Those days were long gone, having been replaced by adult tragedies.

Asia's dark eyes searched his, and he noted the hardness had returned. She took a step back. "I don't feel well," she admitted, then added, "I'm not sure I can handle riding in the enclosed van alone with a stranger."

The small glimpse of her vulnerable side bolstered his protectiveness. "I happen to be down a vehicle. How about if I ride with you and keep you occupied? Distractions help the trip go faster." He used his best conspiratorial tone and said, "Plus, it'll delay the report I have to write about my car's demise."

Asia shrugged without comment, but relief softened the lines on her forehead. Slade took the token of acceptance and helped her to the ambulance. "I need to confer with my sergeant. Then I'll accompany Mrs. Stratton to the hospital," he told Hereford, who grunted his acknowledgment.

"One minute," Slade assured Asia.

She waved him off, and he returned to where Oliver, Trey and the deputies stood inspecting his damaged patrol unit. Slade provided a brief recap of the events, starting with Nevil Quenten's DOA status—temporarily omitting the significant detail of Asia's gun possession—emphasizing her injuries and then concluding with the shoot-out in the shed.

Oliver pulled himself to his full six-foot-two-inch height and addressed the team. "Thank you for responding. Set up a perimeter." He turned to Trey. "Have K9 Magnum search the property. Mark whatever you find with flags, but do not touch it. We'll let the evidence techs handle collection."

"Affirmative." Trey strode to his pickup and released his police service dog, Magnum, from the cab. The Belgian Malinois barked his appreciation, and the duo navigated to the rear of the home, where they'd work a spiral search pattern of the exterior, starting outside the shed.

Oliver continued issuing the directives, but his voice faded into the background. Slade's focus returned to Asia, sitting at the rear of the ambulance as the paramedic dressed her wound.

The two deputies sprinted past him, yanking Slade to the present as they sped off the property.

Now was his chance to buy Asia some time with his boss. Slade moved quickly to where Oliver stood alone, typing into his cell phone. "Sir?"

The sergeant finished his entry before looking up.

"I can't believe Asia—er, Mrs. Stratton—would commit murder. It's obvious she's in danger and needs our help."

Oliver slipped his phone into his belt clip. "You don't have to pretend she's a stranger. I'm aware of the friendship you and Zander once had, including the fact the three of you were childhood classmates."

Slade and Asia had been more than classmates, but Oliver didn't need to know any of those details.

"Right. I respectfully request time to gather more intel before making any hasty decisions."

"You mean you don't want to arrest her."

"I don't want to *prematurely* arrest her. The stigma of a cop's wife committing murder…"

"The press and public would bake her. I understand and agree. However, I'm still confused as to how you ended up here in the first place."

"That's a little trickier to explain. I received a text from Asia's number asking for help, with a map screenshot of this location."

"She lured you here?" Oliver's tone hardened.

Slade withdrew his cell phone and displayed the message. "She insists she never sent the text. It came from her number, but that doesn't prove the sender."

Oliver shook his head. "You said Quenten was already DOA?"

"Yes, sir." Slade hesitated.

"Did she have defensive wounds?"

"She's got injuries, possibly defensive, but she's unsure how they occurred."

"She's claiming amnesia?"

Slade shifted from one foot to the other. "Partially. Asia said the last thing she recalls is being in her apartment on Thursday. She's got no recollection of arriving here or the time in between."

Oliver's expression gave no indication as to whether he believed Slade. "Quenten's got enough enemies. Start at her home. Perhaps returning to a familiar place will help trigger her memory. One more thing." Oliver stepped closer and lowered his voice. "The clock is ticking. We'll help Asia in every way possible, but we will not ignore the law. She's our only suspect, and unless something drastic changes in the next seventy-two hours, she must be brought in for questioning."

Slade understood the rationale. Seventy-two hours for the processing of evidence. A short span of time. "I understand. Guess I'd better call in a tow for my car."

Oliver shook his head. "No, I'll handle that. If these men are looking for something, they'll try again, and I want them caught. Whoever brought Asia here had a specific reason."

"Yes, sir."

"Do not let her out of your sight. If she's guilty, we'll have to deal with it by the book. But if she's not, she'll need all the help we can provide. She's still blue family."

Asia needed them, even if she was too stubborn to admit it. If he were honest with himself, there was a part of Slade that needed her too. This was his chance to make up for destroying her life by turning in Zander. He didn't want to arrest her, but if it came down to that, he'd do so, while protecting her within guidelines. Then he'd prove her innocence because there was no way she was guilty.

He'd almost guarantee it… Almost.

An unmarked navy blue truck approached and parked on the other side of Trey's K9 pickup, blocking Slade's view of the driver.

"Trooper, we need to go," Hereford called.

Slade sprinted to the ambulance, where Asia sat propped up and unrestrained on the stretcher. An IV line trailed from her wrist. "I'm fine," she groused. "This is unnecessary."

The EMT grinned and stepped aside, giving Slade and Asia privacy. Slade leaned in and whispered, "It's this or riding in the special visitor seat of a patrol car."

She pressed her lips into a flat line. "Point taken."

Slade walked toward Hereford. "I need to wrap a few things up with my sergeant. Can you give me two minutes? Will she be okay?"

He nodded. "She's lost a lot of blood but she's stable. One minute."

"Thanks." Slade returned to where Detective Kent Beardly now joined Oliver.

Of all people, why had Oliver chosen him? Slade couldn't work the crime scene, which was reasonable, but the last thing they needed was another hand in the mix. Beardly's cop skills were decent, but he had all the finesse of a longhorn bull. Slade stood undecided between leaving Beardly to assume the investigation and accompanying Asia to the hospital.

Beardly faced Slade with a clenched jaw, as if he'd interrupted an important meeting. "Mrs. Stratton's claiming amnesia? A little cliché, don't you think?"

Had the man's voice always been that gravelly? Agitation and defensiveness sent Slade's hackles up. "It's possible, but after the shoot-out we endured, it's more than probable she's telling the truth. Says she's lost the past two days." Slade kept Asia in view.

Beardly tsked, shaking his head. "Haven't seen her since the funeral. Heard she'd pretty much disappeared afterward. Not inconceivable she's using like Zander."

Slade gritted his teeth, not wanting to participate in Beardly's attempt at gossip.

Thankfully, Oliver regained command of the conversation. "We haven't assessed the scene yet. Asia's obviously got enemies. She's innocent until proven guilty. Jackson, provide her protective detail at the hospital."

"Sarge, with all due respect, Jackson's too close to this." Beardly slapped a palm on Slade's shoulder. "No offense."

None taken, and no one asked you. Slade restrained the urge to swat Beardly's hand away.

The detective continued, "It'd be better to have an impartial party do the detail."

No way. If he had to do it incognito, Slade wasn't letting Asia out of his sight. If she recovered her memory with the wrong people, she'd be dead for sure.

"With all due respect," he mimicked, "I'm without a car. Asia is claustrophobic, and I promised to ride with her. She trusts me." *Liar.* "I'd like the detail." Did he sound too eager?

"Trooper, we need to get Mrs. Stratton to the hospital," the taller paramedic said.

"When she's released, we'll determine continued custody at that time. Jackson, go with Asia. Beardly, lead the investigation here," Oliver asserted.

Beardly squared his shoulders and puffed out his chest. "You can count on me, sir. No two-bit criminal goes after one of our blue family and gets away with it."

All the overexuberant detective needed now was to don

a cape and leggings. Slade spun on his heel and sprinted for the ambulance.

"If Mrs. Stratton remembers anything that might help us, contact me immediately," Beardly called.

Slade rolled his eyes, climbed into the rig and dropped onto the metal bench. Hereford sat across from them charting Asia's vitals, while the other EMT took the driver's seat. Within seconds, they rumbled off the property.

They passed Oliver. He stood several feet away, gesturing with wide, emphatic movements to a new set of responding officers from multiple surrounding agencies. A call for an officer-involved shooting brought out everyone. Even with a tight perimeter and law enforcement presence, Slade doubted they'd catch the criminals. If only the team had arrived a few minutes sooner.

Was Asia faking her selective amnesia? She'd been an angry, defensive woman, but she'd never been a liar. However, desperation motivated people to make foolish choices.

"How're you doing?" Slade broke the silence.

Asia bit her lip. "Do you think any of this has to do with Zander?"

Sure, now she wants to divulge in front of a stranger. Slade glanced at Hereford, who busied himself with paperwork. "I can't help but consider the possibility of a connection." He'd prefer not to have this conversation in the man's company. Still, letting her talk might work better than interrogating her.

Asia twirled the white sheet around her fingers, and the childlike motion reminded him of his two-year-old niece. "I haven't asked for updates on his investigation since the funeral. I couldn't deal with it, but I can't hide from it anymore. Especially with this happening. I need to understand what's going on. Have there been any leads in Zander's case?" she asked.

Slade leaned closer. She didn't move away, and the momentary acceptance touched him. Maybe she'd forgive him someday—though he didn't deserve it, and he'd never ask. He shifted under the weight of discussing the investigation. Memories of Zander's crime scene and broken body sent an involuntary shiver up his spine. How much should he share? Struggling to find the right words, he determined to be honest while revealing only what was necessary. "There's been no progress—"

"Oh." Asia fell back against the stretcher and pinched the bridge of her nose. "I'm so nauseous."

"You may have a concussion," Hereford advised.

"We'll talk later. Just rest." Slade reached for Asia's arm, then retracted his hand. By the book and professional was the only way he could truly help her. Even if she never forgave him for Zander's death.

The swaying and bumping of the ambulance across the gravel roads worsened Asia's nausea, swirling her stomach into knots. She leaned against the cool sheet covering the stretcher and closed her eyes while fisting the metal frame. Nothing relieved the dizziness. She swallowed hard and inhaled deeply to calm herself.

A shiver crept up her spine at the recollection of Nevil Quenten's lifeless black eyes. *Lord, I need Your help. How do I prove I'm innocent when all they see is my guilt?*

And who could blame them? If she were on the outside looking in, she'd feel the same way. Except she was on the inside looking out, and she was no killer. Asia pressed her fingers against her forehead. The drumming in her brain intensified, and she squeezed her eyes tighter, concentrating on her prayers rather than the discomfort.

The plethora of self-condemning questions continued to ravage her mind. Why hadn't she run away when she'd come to? What possessed her to grab the gun? How stupid was she? Her train wreck of a life had spiraled out of control, and now her only hope of proving her innocence was to find Nevil Quenten's real murderer. Would that also prove who had murdered Zander? They were obviously connected. But why drag her into it?

Guilt hit her. Why had she asked about Zander's case? The familiar juxtaposition of love and sorrow swirled in her memories of her deceased husband. In a short time, she'd gone through a full range of emotions from terror to humiliation. Was there any way off this crazy train?

"Are you feeling better?"

Asia opened her eyes and faced Slade. "I doubt that'll happen unless this is all a horrible nightmare, and I wake up."

"Did you want to call someone?"

Like who? The rock in her throat threatened to cut off her air supply, and the only faces she pictured were her parents'. Asia concentrated on the sheet until it blurred as she tried to silence the condemning mantra. *If only I hadn't been so selfish, they wouldn't be dead.*

Zander's outward charismatic personality and intimate neediness had compelled her to follow him to the University of Nebraska in Lincoln. Mom's and Daddy's quiet natures and gentle understanding provided all the approval Asia needed. They promised to visit often and had kept that promise, even when blizzard warnings covered every news channel that lethal night. Daddy had assured Asia the storm wouldn't be an issue, but they'd never anticipated the wrecked semi jackknifed across the highway. Invisible arrows penetrated her heart with each agonizing image.

"I wasn't sure if you had a friend or someone you'd like to notify," Slade clarified, invading her misery.

She turned away. "There's no one." The bitter words stung

her throat. "Not that you'd ever understand being alone." Asia didn't meet Slade's eyes. Couldn't. His family—a raucous, close-knit group where love and laughter enveloped everyone in a ten-mile radius—had been her second home. A family she'd betrayed for Zander.

The memories increased the burn in her chest and hollow ache in her heart. She and Zander had always been a volatile combination. Her nurturing instincts combined with his lack of family—thanks to his mother's drug overdose—entangled them in an isolating solace of false peace. Zander's eventual emotional and physical abandonment left Asia more alone than she'd ever thought possible. Only superficial work relationships existed for her.

Work. One more consideration. Asia studied her fingernails. "I returned to the salon two weeks ago, and I have no vacation time. They'll fire me." She turned to Slade. "Unless..."

"Unless?"

"Do you think I'll be able to go home by tomorrow morning?" It was stupid to even hope for such a thing, and the doubt in Slade's eyes spoke his answer. "Never mind. Doesn't matter," she mumbled.

"Don't want you losing your job."

"Yeah, well, one missed paycheck won't change my meager lifestyle," she said, miffed that she'd revealed too much. *A prison sentence would eliminate the need for employment, anyway.*

Slade appeared taken aback. "Are you having financial troubles? I assumed Zander's insurance—"

"Not that it's any of your business." Asia drilled him with her best you-asked-for-it scowl. "But I never received any money. Turns out, they withhold life-insurance benefits when there's an ongoing investigation." Slade's invasive comment meant he was digging. The department mandated every trooper carry life insurance of at least two times their salary.

He grimaced and swallowed. "I'm sorry. I didn't realize… but you had the house? Equity after the sale?"

She shook her head. "The bank foreclosed on our house when I failed to pay the second mortgage Zander forged in my name. Of course, that was right after he'd cleaned out our savings." Why was she confessing her financial woes to him? It was none of Slade's concern, and the EMT looked like he wanted to crawl under her stretcher and hide.

"Zander's path of destruction had no boundaries," Slade murmured.

Asia started to defend her deceased husband but lost the energy to follow through. She reached up and gently touched the tender spot on her head, allowing her fingers to graze the hard, crusty sections of her hair where blood had coagulated. Another unknown, though surely in her favor. She couldn't have inflicted the injury to herself.

Slade leaned closer. "I wasn't aware things were so difficult. Why didn't you call me? I would've helped you."

She crossed her arms, blinked and tilted her head. "Why would I run to *you*?"

The words were harsh, but Slade's nonchalant manner surprised her. "To be honest, my thoughts exactly. You've never asked for my help. Which made your text tonight even more baffling."

So we're back to quizzing me. "Someone else sent that message. Find my phone and I'll prove it." Her voice sounded far more confident than the fear swarming her heart. The more disturbing question was, how had the killer connected her and Slade? They hadn't talked since the funeral, and even that had been strained.

She considered him. After all they'd been through this evening, he'd maintained his perfectly put-together self.

Examining her blouse and pants, she grimaced. *I, on the other hand, resemble a demolition-derby car.*

Slade pulled out his notepad and wrote something down. "What did the message say?"

"Hmm?" He glanced up from his note taking.

"The text you're accusing me of sending. What did it say?" she repeated.

Slade withdrew his cell phone, scrolled through his messages and passed the device to her. Asia's name and number appeared in the contact area along with her picture. A print screen showed a map and one word—Help.

She studied the words and image, using her fingers to zoom in closer. "Is this where we were?"

He quirked an eyebrow. "Yes."

She handed him the phone. "I never sent the message, and I don't recognize the address."

He dismissed her by slipping the device into his belt clip. "For the record, you could've asked for my help."

An unladylike snort escaped, and she shifted her gaze.

"I didn't want to report Zander. It was—"

Asia jerked to face him, and the headache gained new rhythm behind her eyeballs. "What, Slade?" She cut him off. "The right thing to do?"

Tension covered his expression, and his posture stiffened. Satisfaction at silencing him reminded her of their disconnected relationship. He wasn't her friend. He'd lost that privilege a long time ago, and she'd never give him the chance to hurt her again.

Slade palmed the notepad. "I realize you weren't able to see them from your vantage point, but did you recognize either of those men? Their voices?"

Without hesitation, Asia responded with an emphatic head shake. "Not at all."

"What do you know about the deceased?" Slade refrained from using Quenten's name. Did he not trust the EMT? Or was he testing her?

"Limited comments from Zander, but nothing of significance." Her mind raced, and questions tumbled out fast, crashing over one another. "Why would a guy like him come after me? Why are those men looking for me? What do they want?"

Slade worked his jaw and gave a slight shake of his head. This wasn't the place to discuss Nevil Quenten or Zander. Not to mention, something about his mannerisms suggested he didn't believe her. The darkened expression on his rugged face sent a tremor of worry through Asia. Was she becoming paranoid in her efforts to prove her innocence?

"We'll figure this out."

His calm manner should have been comforting. Instead, it irked her. Did he not comprehend the problem? The danger she faced? Or did he not care?

"If they're searching for me, they'll find me. Why was I there with that—that—criminal?" Asia spit the last word, then continued, "How did they know I was there? Where have I been? How did I get there?" Frustration made her ramble, leaving no opening for Slade to respond. "What is going on?"

The walls of the ambulance closed in, reminding Asia she was a prisoner with the ever-watchful Slade. He'd never let her out of his sight, yet the sudden urge to jump up and thrust open the doors tempted her. Common sense revealed the impossibility of the option—it was something out of an action movie, not real-life drama.

Her heart rate quickened, and the EMT shifted his gaze to the monitor. "Ma'am, please calm down."

Asia worried her lip. *I have done nothing wrong.* True enough, but the truth had paled when the other officers arrived, and the terror of her reality hit again. And of course,

Sergeant Oliver and Slade's brother Trey would be the responding troopers. It would've been easier to deal with two strangers than a reunion of her deceased husband's coworkers. Not that they'd hung out and been friends. An unexpected wave of sadness washed over her. She'd lost so much with Zander's death. Even the identity of being part of the patrol family. They wouldn't be amicable once they arrested her for murder.

"We'll get to the bottom of this," Slade repeated, though it held no promise for her freedom. The wretched ringing of his cell phone interrupted the conversation.

Asia watched his expression as he answered the call. The crease in his forehead said the news wasn't good. He disconnected and met her eyes.

"What's wrong?" Her pulse quickened as each silent second ticked by.

"Let's talk later."

Common sense said to keep quiet; this wasn't the time or place. Asia ignored her instinct and blurted, "No. Tell me now."

"Later."

His brush-off bothered her. She had the right to be informed of every detail of her case. "Slade, I can take whatever you have to say."

He sighed, and Asia jerked to look at the EMT, who avoided her gaze. Slade leaned closer and spoke in a barely audible volume. "Magnum found cocaine in your purse."

She gripped the stretcher's rails to keep from jumping up. "No! That's not possible. I don't… It wasn't my purse, then!"

"The investigators also discovered your wallet and phone inside."

"Whatever they *think* they found, it wasn't mine."

Slade shook his head. Disbelief? Preoccupation? "There's more. The CSIs identified the gun at the scene."

She swallowed, and her heartbeat pounded in her ears. "That was fast."

"The state patrol emblem was inscribed on the side with a badge number."

Asia held her breath, dreading the next words.

"It was Zander's service weapon."

No. "But the investigators took all of his equipment after…" Asia paused midargument. Why would she have his gun? Zander always kept it in his possession, and he hadn't lived with her for over a year. The department collected all his issued items. She'd refused to go to his apartment, but they'd told her everything had been cleaned out. Why hadn't she confirmed?

"Zander's weapon went missing before his murder," Slade clarified.

Asia's shoulders tightened. "You can't seriously believe I killed Nevil Quenten using Zander's gun? Or that I was running drugs? Slade, come on."

He seemed to age before her eyes. "I don't know."

Asia gritted her teeth. What didn't he know? *Whether I'm a murderer? Whether I'm lying now?* The three words plagued her from every angle. She didn't know how she'd gotten here, and her only ally didn't know if he believed her. Wretched irony.

THREE

Fatigue wore through Slade's depleting energy reserves. His phone buzzed, dragging him into consciousness, and a glance at the screen revealed it was 02:34 in the morning. He repositioned in the uncomfortable hospital chair. The night seemed to stretch on forever. Asia had endured multiple tests on machines with names resembling alphabet soup, and finally the surgery to repair her shoulder. Thankfully, the bullet had missed her vital organs and arteries.

Slade scrubbed his palm over his face, then read Oliver's demand for an update. Based on the tone, he'd avoided the conversation with his boss for one message too long. He'd hoped to receive the lab results first, but it was time to confront the inevitable.

The phone buzzed again. "Give me a minute," Slade groused in a whispered reply to the inanimate object.

Asia sighed and rolled over, reminding him to be quiet. She appeared to sleep peacefully, and he didn't want to wake her. The poor woman needed rest.

He glanced down, expecting Oliver's number, but a new text message from his friend's wife—a manager in the hospital lab—resuscitated his hope. Asia's tox results confirmed the presence of scopolamine. A drug Quenten's cronies specialized in because it kept the victim conscious and compliant, but blocked memory formation.

Renewed optimism had Slade slipping from Asia's hospital room. The scopolamine explained Asia's temporary amnesia and added plausible deniability about her participation in Quenten's death. Unease crept between Slade's shoulder blades. Oliver would demand an answer as to how Slade had obtained the rapid results. The reality of him facing disciplinary action for unlawful use of authority was a serious consideration. He didn't want to get his friend's wife in trouble, but the evidence helped Asia's defense. *Please don't let Oliver ask for details.* The prayer escaped before Slade debated whether God would frown on such a request.

Lacey Fisher, the young female trooper Sergeant Oliver assigned to assist with Asia's security, sat in the hallway keeping watch. She glanced up, acknowledging Slade as he palmed his phone. "Please sit with Mrs. Stratton. She's asleep. I'll be back in five minutes. I need to make a call, but the reception in the hospital's terrible."

"Affirmative." Fisher jumped to her feet.

He waited until the trooper entered Asia's room, then strode through the gray hallway where pictures of farming landscapes hung at two-foot intervals. The path curved and disappeared behind him toward the elevators. He poked the down arrow and exhaled, allowing the night's events to loom in his mind.

The ride to the lobby ended too soon. Slade traipsed through the vacant area to the hospital's electric glass entry. He shivered as the frosty air greeted him. With a tap to Oliver's contact icon, he made the call and exited the building.

"Glad to see you found time to report in. What's Mrs. Stratton's status?" Oliver barked without saying hello.

His sergeant's comments were deserved and expected, but Slade cringed anyway. Avoiding the man didn't rank high on the smart-things-to-do list, but procrastination came easy to him. "She's resting now. Doctor stitched up the bullet wound, but the concussion and her blood pressure have him wanting to keep her overnight for observation."

Oliver exhaled into the receiver. "That's a relief. No need to rush her departure. The CSIs have finished for the night. They won't release the scene until they've had a chance to go over it again in the morning with better lighting."

Slade contemplated asking his next question, then concluded they had to know everything Asia faced. "Sir, did they find anything else—"

"You mean besides a dead cartel leader, murder weapon, her purse and the drugs?" Oliver snapped.

The gun hadn't been confirmed as the murder weapon, but correcting his boss would be unwise. "Something like that."

"Nothing of significance. I've requested her phone records because her cell is password protected. Should have them within a few hours."

Slade heard the veiled implication. Unless the killer had her password, it appeared Asia had sent the text. Would the records help her case or make it worse? Why hadn't she dialed 9-1-1?

"The drugs in Asia's purse require her arrest. At the very least, she must be detained for questioning and processing."

"But you said her purse was found in one of the bedroom closets. A good attorney will refute the evidence since the purse wasn't actively in her possession." Slade's weak argument was the best he could muster at the late hour.

"True, but the murder charges aren't as avoidable. Doubtful he shot himself, Trooper."

"Yes, sir. That part is a little harder to rebut."

"Once the lab fingerprints the weapon…"

Slade swallowed hard. Asia's prints were all over the gun. The realization left him reeling. Whether she was drugged or not, if the clothes he'd submitted had gunshot residue on them, it would only add to the evidence against her. Even without the ballistics report, there was little doubt in his mind that the bullet that killed Quenten came from Zander's weapon. The same one Asia had been holding. "They'll find Asia's prints on the gun."

"I see. You'd better start over and tell me *exactly* what happened before my arrival." Oliver's impatience oozed through the line.

Everything within Slade wanted to circumvent the truth, but there was no pretending or denying she'd held the gun. Until now, he hadn't offered those specifics. With a sigh, he recounted the story again, this time including all the pertinent information, and ended with the men fleeing at the sirens.

"That's a significant omitted detail." Oliver's tone, though agitated, wasn't irate. "I suppose there's the possibility that Quenten attacked her first."

Perhaps his boss would give Asia the benefit of the doubt. "Then it would be self-defense." Slade inhaled and launched into his practiced speech informing Oliver about the scopolamine.

Oliver's pause hung between them for so long that Slade held his breath, expecting the worst. "I see. I'm not even going to ask how you obtained results that quickly."

Whew. "Sir, Quenten should also be tested for drugs. Something that might explain immobility? How else was he shot square in the forehead? There are seasoned troopers who lack that type of accuracy. I'm sure there's more to this than we're seeing. It would be easy to book her and call it a done deal, but my gut says Asia's innocent. What if the murderer's intention was to lure me there and take out both of us?"

"Don't get ahead of yourself. Listen, I'm not heartless. I feel for her. Asia's had a full plate longer than anyone should have to. I'll request the tox screen on Quenten. In the meantime, ensure she's safe and keep me posted." Oliver disconnected.

Relief and a second wind had Slade rushing through the hospital doors. He paced in front of the elevator while his brain raced out of control. He had hope again, and that was huge. Dad always said hope was like blinders on a horse—it focused a man's attention and eliminated his peripheral vision. Of course, he'd been talking about falling in love, not battling murder charges. If only they had a clue in her favor.

All of this was connected to Zander. Even in death the guy hurt Asia, and he'd never deserved her. Although Slade had ample opportunities to tattle about Zander's extramarital activities, he refused to break Asia's heart. He'd also feared losing her friendship, or worse, having her hate him. *Oh wait, I've accomplished that. Score one for overachievers.*

Slade punched the elevator button again, rehashing Oliver's instructions.

Asia deserved justice. That was his sole objective, and if they found her guilty, he would do what was required of him. But only if and/or when he was certain, beyond any reasonable doubt. He wanted facts and evidence—neither had anything to do with personal feelings. Slade had buried those long ago.

The elevator dinged like a timer on his thoughts, and the doors opened. Slade's heart was convinced of Asia's innocence, and maybe—just maybe—proving it would ease the guilt that had haunted him since Zander's death.

He'd failed once to save a life. Never again.

* * *

"Hello, Mrs. Stratton," a man's voice hissed in greeting.

Asia jerked upright in the hospital bed, stopped short by the bindings encircling her wrists and ankles. Pain radiated up her shoulder, and something covered her mouth, muting her cry. Terror gripped her chest, a tightening vise that restricted each breath. Against common sense, she tugged harder. The burning sensation confirmed her escape efforts had torn through her skin while the restraints remained unrelenting.

"It is useless to fight." The baritone voice sent a shiver down Asia's spine.

Streetlamps outside cast dim light through the partially closed slats of the white plastic blinds. Asia blinked, willing her eyes to focus in the dark. She scanned the room in search of the intruder. How had he gotten in? Where was Slade?

Her perusal stopped short on the form in the corner chair. The same place where Slade had perched all evening. Now a woman sat slumped there. Recognition came to Asia—the female trooper assigned outside her door. Frazer? No, Fisher.

Asia froze, and her muffled gasp caught in the sticky substance covering her mouth. She inhaled the stench of glue, and sharp edges pulled the tender skin near her nostrils. Tape. Relieved the person wasn't Slade, she prayed Fisher was unconscious and not dead.

"Cooperate and this will go well for you. I do not want to hurt you."

Asia turned and startled at the black gorilla mask inches from her face.

"Your husband was a stupid man. He could've survived if he'd given us the card. Make a smarter choice and I'll let you live. Tell me where it is." The man crept around the foot of her bed, sliding his fingers along the white blanket.

Card? What was he talking about? She blinked several times. Had she heard him correctly? Asia's mind raced. Since the intruder had disguised himself, that must mean he had no intention of killing her since she couldn't identify him. But what card did he want?

He stepped toward the trooper and pressed a hand against the woman's shoulder. "It's too bad the cops are incapable of protecting you. But that's the kind of danger you're up against."

Asia's breaths came faster, caught in the tape. The threats sent fear oozing through her veins. She shoved against the bed with her heels, digging the plastic restraints harder into her skin. What would he do to her to get the information he wanted? Terrifying images passed through her mind. *Please, God, help me!*

Fight! The word bounced to the forefront of Asia's brain, giving her the snap-out-of-it kick she needed. *Think.* The creep would have to remove the tape in order for her to speak, and when he did, she'd scream with everything in her.

Asia forced herself to inhale through her nose and commanded her racing heart to obey. A sliver of light shone beneath the closed door. Would anyone hear her? *Where are you, Slade?* She sensed impending doom, but annoyance pricked at the corners of her mind, providing momentary relief from her fear. He'd let her down again and proved, once more, Slade Jackson could not be counted upon.

The gorilla-masked man returned to Asia's side. "Are you ready to talk?"

He ran a finger along her cheek, jolting her back to the present. The quick movement perpetuated the agony in her shoulder, coordinating a throbbing rhythm with her heart-beat. She groaned.

The man tsked. "Careful. Don't hurt yourself."

Darkness disguised the intruder, and only his heavy breathing reverberated beside her. Sweat beaded on her forehead, trickling down her face.

The man leaned closer, his dark eyes unblinking behind the gorilla mask's eye holes. "I'm making a good-faith effort by keeping my identity hidden. Once I remove the tape, you'll have one chance to return the favor." His voice was muffled by the mask. "If you scream, I'll kill you. I only want the card, Mrs. Stratton. Do we understand each other?"

Fury and fear warred within Asia, and she stubbornly refused to break away from his gaze. She'd call his bluff because the man wanted something more than he wanted her dead; otherwise he'd have killed her while she slept. That was her assurance. At least she prayed that was true. Her gaze drifted to the trooper slumped in the chair as confirmation. *Please let her be alive.*

Asia returned her eyes to the masked man. She had no clue about this card he referred to, but he seemed convinced she possessed it. She nodded and her cooperative gesture had the assailant patting her head like a dog. "Good girl."

He moved to the right, remaining in the shadows.

She flattened her hand under the blanket, ignoring the burn in her injured shoulder and allowing her fingers to roam.

She grazed an object. He hadn't taken the bed's remote control! Asia slid her palm over the box, keeping her body as still as possible. There were several buttons. Which would call the nurse? If she pressed the wrong switch, it would send her bed's foot or head into motion and eliminate any chance for help. Two toggles. Those must move the bed. Fingering the device, she searched for a single button and paused.

"Remember, I will give you only one opportunity to tell me where the card is." He returned to her side and flipped open a switchblade, then pressed the cold steel along her neck.

Asia sucked in a breath and pressed the button on the remote. *Lord, please let this be the right one.* There was a *ding*, followed by a red light illuminated on the power pad above her bed.

The man jerked then met her gaze with a venomous glare. "You'll pay for that."

Asia squeezed her eyes shut, preparing for the worst.

He launched into a myriad of curses before bolting from the room.

Slade exited the elevator to the sound of a woman's scream. He sprinted down the hallway, and the nurse ran to meet him. "A man wearing a gorilla mask just ran through those doors." She gestured to the stairwell.

Slade quickened his pace and shoved open the door. His boots thudded against the thick plastic floor as he took two and three steps at a time, gripping the rail for support. The rapid staccato rhythm of footsteps echoed as Slade hurried after the intruder.

The man was at least a level ahead of him and gaining speed.

A slam below indicated he'd exited the stairwell.

Slade jumped over the railing onto the main floor and burst through the door into the garage.

The squealing of tires reverberated throughout the cement walls. A dark SUV skidded out of the building, its red taillights mocking the chase.

He'd been so close! Slade slammed his hand on the wall,

then spun on his heel and pressed the button on his shoulder mic. "Intruder escaped. Put out an APB on a black SUV, newer model, no plates, headed southbound from the hospital garage."

The dispatcher responded but her words were inconsequential. Once again, the criminal had evaded arrest.

Yanking the door open, Slade nearly collided with the female security guard on the other side.

She stepped back, eyes wide in question.

"He got away. I'll need to see your security footage."

"Yes, sir."

He passed her and jogged up the steps with the guard trailing behind.

"We can view the video in my office," she called.

"Negative. Bring it to room 422. I'm staying with my witness." *Since I nearly got her killed by leaving her.*

Slade didn't wait for the guard's response or for her to catch up. He threw open the door to the fourth floor and ran down the hall.

Trooper Lacey Fisher lay on a stretcher, and an orderly pushed her from Asia's room into the hallway.

Slade increased his pace. "Excuse me."

The man paused.

"Is she okay?"

"Unconscious but breathing," the orderly answered, then resumed his mission, moving past Slade.

Thank God. Fisher was alive.

Torn between following the orderly and checking on Asia, Slade chose to receive Asia's well-deserved rebuke. She could've been killed thanks to his lackadaisical approach to her security, and he'd learned a valuable lesson. Whatever it took, he needed to remain at her side, because whoever had their target locked on Asia Stratton would stop at nothing to get to her.

* * *

Asia focused on the nurse's name tag, which read *Ramona*, as she snipped through the plastic ties. In her peripheral, she saw Slade enter the room and halt by the door.

The pounding pulse beating in her ears muted the woman's soft words, and she captured only, "You're safe now."

"I'll never be safe." Speaking the words aloud solidified their truth for Asia.

"You'll be fine," Nurse Ramona assured her. "They'll catch the man." She gathered the remnants of the restraints and turned to leave.

Doubtful. Lack of patience had Asia throwing her legs over the edge of the bed.

In a two-stride movement, Ramona impeded Asia's escape, sporting a no-nonsense frown and rooted stance. All hesitation left the nurse's voice. "You will stay in your bed and allow the police to deal with the intruder." Though she was petite, the woman's confident demeanor said she'd give Asia a literal run for her money if she tried to leave the room. "The safest place for you is right here."

"But I—"

"Please, Mrs. Stratton." Ramona pulled back the covers and waited as Asia stood awkwardly next to the bed. "You don't want to tear open your stitches." She didn't move until Asia had obeyed and tucked her legs under the blankets. "I'll return in a second to dress your wounds." She pointed for emphasis to the thin red welts and beads of crimson engraving Asia's skin.

"Fine." Asia slumped against the pillows.

The nurse gave an approving nod and headed out of the room.

"When you've got a moment, would you please provide an update on Trooper Fisher?" Slade asked.

"Of course." She closed the door softly behind her.

Slade approached, concern written on his red face.

The lines surrounding his caramel eyes conveyed compassion, and his muscular chest heaved from exertion. "Did the man hurt you?" He reached to touch her, and she shifted away.

The response came naturally, but whatever Asia read in his expression—defeat or frustration—left her unsettled, almost sad. "I want to go home." She shivered and drew her knees up, wrapping her arms around them. "He threatened to kill me if I didn't give him a card. I don't know what he's talking about!"

Slade stepped back, crossing his arms over his chest. "Did you recognize him?"

"Not at all. He wore a gorilla mask the whole time and said he was making a good-faith effort by not letting me see his face."

Slade scowled. "He got away, for now. Security is compiling the camera footage and I've got an APB on him."

What difference would an all-points bulletin make? Asia studied him. Would he help her? "You have to get me out of here."

Uncrossing his arms, Slade shook his head. "No, the doctors want to watch you overnight."

"How about what I want? Like to stay alive?" She lowered her voice and gripped the sheet. "I have to prove I didn't kill Quenten and find that stupid card! Maybe they'll leave me alone once I hand it over."

"They won't allow you to go skipping off into the sunset. They'll kill you once they have what they want."

"Then help me!"

Slade shifted at her bedside. "I am and will continue doing everything possible to help you. Whatever it takes, I will protect you."

Classic Slade, with his kind and thoughtful words, but

he didn't understand. Asia shook her head. Procedure Boy would never step outside the box, and right now, playing by the rules might get her killed.

"You can't protect me. No one can." She shoved off the blankets and swung her feet over the side.

"I cannot allow you to leave." Slade grasped her uninjured arm, his restraint gentle but strong.

Asia looked up at him. "Let go of me." The faded scent of aftershave wafted to her, drawing attention to Slade's neck. He flexed his jaw, then released his hold, still blocking her from climbing out of the bed. She sat with her feet swinging childlike above the cold linoleum floor.

"I'll be right by your side. I won't leave for anything. I promise."

But his promise wouldn't save her. "Then what? I can't stay here forever."

"When the doctor releases you, I'll—"

"—be forced to arrest me?" she concluded.

He looked down. "Not if I can find evidence to help you."

"I'm not naive. If the man found me in a hospital with an armed guard—who he knocked out, by the way—he'll locate me anywhere. You might as well hand me over to those men, because if you put me in prison, I'll have no defense. You'll be delivering me to them on a department-of-corrections platter."

He met her gaze and seemed to consider her protest before spouting, "I can't ignore the law."

And there it was—the assurance Slade Jackson would not remain true to his promise to protect her. His definition of *anything* did not include breaking the law, even if it saved her life. Asia forced herself not to roll her eyes and remained calm. Hysteria wouldn't work for coercion. "I know. But you can give me a chance to get away."

Slade sighed, rubbing his hand over his neck, unnerving her with his hesitancy. "The evidence looks really bad. If you take off, you'll look guiltier. Innocent people don't run."

She harrumphed. "Terrorized innocent people do."

"Touché." One side of his mouth tilted upward in a grin but quickly faded. "Where would you go?"

She ignored the question, unwilling to share any details. Mostly because, at the moment, she had no clue. "Do *you* believe me?"

"That's irrelevant."

"No, it's not."

He didn't reply. Asia fisted her hands and pushed off the bed. Slade stood in her way, so she remained where she was. "This is insane. I'm the victim here, and I'm the one being accused. You've known me since we were kids. After our history together, how can you wonder if I'm guilty?"

Slade's gaze flicked upward, and he exhaled loudly. "Stop jumping to conclusions. Besides, my opinion isn't important. It won't help you at all in front of a judge or a jury."

Why was the man talking in circles? It may be unfair to remind him of their connection, but desperation was making her toss fairness out the window. Slade had always been her defender, from the time they were in kindergarten and little Lenny Miller had stolen her pencil and refused to give it back. Now when it mattered most, he wasn't on her side?

Asia clenched her fists, frustration building. "It matters to me. You know me, probably better than anyone, and if you don't believe me, why should anyone else?" She clamped her mouth shut. Why had she said that?

Slade frowned, furrowing his eyebrows. "I never said I don't believe you."

"You also never said you do."

He planted his feet in a wide stance. "We have a little time before I have to take you in for questioning. Let's use it wisely to figure things out. There's still a chance I won't have to arrest you. We can start with the drugs they found in your purse. If we can prove they're not yours—"

Tension clutched Asia's shoulders. "They aren't mine! I don't use drugs or drink or anything else. Especially not after everything Zander put me through. I certainly wouldn't be a mule for a dirtbag like Quenten."

"Once the packaging is fingerprinted, the evidence may provide a lead." Slade shifted then leaned against the wall.

Asia slid onto the bed. Her shoulder ached, but she refused to acknowledge the pulsating pain. "Someone set me up with the drugs and Quenten's body."

Slade tilted his head back, averting his eyes. "There's something else. I requested a tox screen."

"What? You don't have any right—"

He held up his hands. "Relax. The lab found a drug called scopolamine in your system."

"I don't understand."

Slade explained how the drug would keep her compliant and prevent her from remembering.

"That's good, right? It proves I'm innocent."

"It's not that easy, but being drugged is in your favor. Let's talk about this card the intruder wanted."

"I haven't got a clue what they're talking about. What kind of card? A greeting card? An identification card? An SD card? A credit card? I don't understand." Asia slapped her hands on the bedding and glared at him. "Look, I'm not asking you to set me free. Just give me a head start to find whatever card they want. It's the only chance I have of proving my innocence. And I'm not going to be able to do anything from here."

Regardless of his answer, she would escape this place.

Out on her own. Being a fugitive couldn't be worse than being an accused murderer. The only person she could depend on was herself. Slade wasn't convinced she was innocent, so he wouldn't help her, and unlike him, she had everything to lose.

"We have to keep this on the up-and-up. No running away."

"I won't try hopping a plane to Mexico to avoid arrest. I'm a lot of things, Slade, but I'm no coward. I will find who killed Nevil Quenten and whoever is trying to frame me. If I die, I die fighting for my life."

"You're not going to die."

"You can't promise that."

"Fair enough, but you're not doing this alone."

"The rules won't—"

"We can do it by the rules."

The man was exasperating. Asia exhaled. "Yeah, how?"

Seconds passed, and a heavy silence hung between them. A dare. Slade paced a small path in front of her, sighed and dropped onto the foot of her bed. Asia scooted her legs away to refrain from kicking him off.

He held her gaze, caramel eyes boring into her. "I'm asking you to trust me and give me time. I'll come up with something."

Asia lifted her chin and folded her arms over her chest. "Think faster, because with or without you, I'm out of here."

FOUR

Asia shifted in the passenger seat of the unmarked patrol car, attempting to get comfortable. Twenty minutes on the road felt more like days. Lack of sleep the night before had left her exhausted and achy. She'd declined the doctor's recommended pain medication for her shoulder. The scheduled meeting with Detective Beardly meant she needed a clear—albeit throbbing—head. But she didn't dare complain aloud.

Her insistence for a break-of-dawn release had required a prolonged debate with her doctor. The effort depleted any scraps left of her waning energy. Still, she'd won, and freedom—however limited it might be—was worth the cost. She wouldn't give Slade any doubts about her leaving the hospital.

"So what's the plan? Are you taking me straight to jail?" She exuded a little more snark than she'd intended, but finesse came with sleep, so she was lacking in both areas.

The corner of Slade's lip curved upward, but his dark sunglasses remained transfixed on the road. "Sergeant Oliver agreed you're in danger and need protective custody. The boldness of last night's attacker proves location is crucial. So we're headed off the grid."

"Where?"

"A safe house."

Based upon the remote highway they traveled, that meant someplace out in middle-of-nowhere Nebraska. A safe house was better than prison, but didn't help solve her case.

"And do what? I can't just sit around. I need to find evidence to exonerate me."

"Agreed. After your meeting with Detective Beardly, Trey and I will review the hospital's video footage again. I want to identify your attacker."

Slade's little brother would join them? That was news to her.

As if in answer, he continued, "Sergeant Oliver authorized Trey to help with your protection detail after Trooper Fisher's attack last night. However, because of low staffing, he added the caveat that Trey might be called out."

Asia snorted. "It's comforting that my personal safety is a patrol priority."

"Your other option is an extended stay at the county jail. There's plenty of law enforcement protection there."

Ouch. She'd meant the comment as a joke. Obviously, she wasn't the only cranky one this morning. "Touché."

Slade frowned. "Sorry, I get grumpy when I'm tired."

"I remember." *Too well.* "Okay…"

"Anyway, then we'll formulate our POA."

She tucked her hands into her hoodie pocket. "Plan of action?"

"I'm impressed you speak acronym." Slade waggled his eyebrows above the rim of his sunglasses, reminding her of the childhood boy she'd known her whole life. The painful reflection of all they'd shared…and all they'd lost.

A tiny chip toppled off the armor around her heart.

Slade's phone rang, and he pulled to the side of the road to take the call. He swiped to answer then shifted the device to his left ear, preventing Asia from overhearing.

The headache intensified to a steady pulse behind her eyes, compounded by the morning sunshine glistening off the snowdrifts that bordered the highway.

"No worries. I can handle it."

She studied him.

"I'm sure it'll be fine. See you soon." He dropped the phone into his coat pocket and pulled back onto the road.

"What was that about?"

"Trey was delayed on a missing-person call."

"Oh." Asia focused on the countryside's miles of rolling hills, separated by the occasional county road or farm. The prior week's snow blanketed the area in an endless wintry landscape. The cold temperatures prevented any significant melting.

Slade flipped on the radio, and a familiar Christmas carol filled the space, eliciting an awkward cheerfulness for the depressing trip.

Dreams of living in the country had once seemed possible. Now Asia was grateful if she earned enough at the salon to pay for her dinky one-bedroom apartment in Newman Valley. What would happen to her?

She had no family, which meant facing her impending incarceration alone. Hopelessness constricted her throat.

Was this all connected to Zander? Their last conversation flowed through her mind. His promises to get clean and stop his incessant marital infidelities. Her stupidity for believing him.

Yet she'd asked Slade to trust her, though the glaring evidence was so condemning it had her almost doubting her own innocence. She sped through her mental index of questions. Whose drugs were in her purse? Who murdered Nevil Quenten? And who had texted Slade? How did they get into her phone?

"My finger," Asia blurted.

"What?"

"I use my fingerprint to unlock my phone." Triumph exploded into hope.

Slade nodded. "That makes sense. The killer could've forced your hand. No pun intended."

Relief coursed through her. "See. I told you I didn't send that text."

"It helps, but we need something more. Between the scopolamine and the killer using your fingerprint to unlock your cell phone, I think we've established plausibility for someone kidnapping and framing you for Quenten's murder."

He'd said *we*. The word brought a measure of comfort to her heart. "You make it sound easy." Maybe she should get an attorney. Asia took a deep breath. "Tell me the truth. Where do I stand? I'm not sure who to call. I don't know any lawyers."

Slade paused. "I'll ask around for recommendations."

Dread clung to her shoulders. He hadn't refuted her need for legal representation. "Am I going to jail?" The words stuck in her throat.

Slade's grip on the steering wheel visibly tightened. "Don't go there. Stay positive. Focus on remembering who else was in the trailer that night. I believe that person pulled the trigger."

"But I can't—" She swallowed.

He worked his jaw. "Asia, the drugs in your purse are enough for an arrest."

Panic tackled her, squeezing the breath from her lungs. "Even if I've never used drugs? Even if they're not mine?"

He didn't reply.

Possession alone would sink her. Asia's mountain of challenges continued to multiply.

Several long silent minutes passed, and a new melody

began with the singer's promise to make it home for Christmas. If only Asia had that reassurance. *Lord, what do I do?*

For the first time, Asia wondered if God was listening.

Slade's attention remained on the road, so he was able to avoid Asia's eyes. He'd never doubted the system and had devoted his life to enforcing the law. So what hindered his confidence now? Fear that Asia would be convicted of a crime she didn't commit?

No. He wouldn't let that happen.

Bolstering his unspoken vow, Slade tilted his head to the side, releasing a satisfying crack and momentary relief from the kink in his neck. Stress still tightened his shoulders, reminding him that he was too old to pull an all-nighter. It'd taken until four o'clock for him to convince Asia not to run. He'd reasoned that if she took off, he'd have no chance of helping her. Being a fugitive would boost her to the top of the suspect list.

She'd finally acquiesced and fallen asleep while he'd kept one eye open and fought to stay awake. He didn't dare give her an opportunity to leave. In a strange way, it pleased him to see this side of Asia. He recognized her feistiness and her relentless will to win the battle. She'd never been a weakling, but years of her deceased husband's neglect had stolen her zeal. Now it returned in her desire to prove her innocence and survive, but anxiety muddled her common sense.

Slade functioned on limited sleep regularly, thanks to the awful recurring dream that stole his slumber. Zander haunted him both in life and death. Until he found the truth behind his friend's murder, he'd relive the nightmare every night.

The buzz of his phone startled him. "Sarge."

"Jackson, what's your ETA?"

"Two minutes. Trey just called. He's on his way too."

"Good. Beardly should be there about the same time."

Slade inhaled and said, "Sir, perhaps we should postpone the interview. There's no rush. It's not like Asia will run away."

Asia harrumphed, crossing her arms. The action was almost cute.

"Don't push it." Apparently, Oliver didn't see the humor. "The interview should've happened last night. Besides, Beardly's not there to arrest her. He's conducting his investigation. Mrs. Stratton is his only witness."

Slade palmed the steering wheel with one hand. "Yes, sir."

"I called to remind you the garage door sometimes sticks. I put the house key in the sedan's glove box."

"Thank you."

"Keep me apprised." Oliver disconnected.

Slade turned off the highway onto the county road and spotted the house on the right. The small ranch encircled by evergreens sat several hundred feet from the road, twenty miles outside the town of Norfolk.

He drove around, giving the property a once-over, then pulled up in front of the single-car garage and pressed the button on the opener. Nothing happened. He tried again, but the door didn't budge. "Great. It's stuck."

"Is that bad?"

"Nah, that's what Oliver called about. You'd think someone would've fixed it by now."

Slade shifted into Park then swiveled to face Asia. "Stay in the car and keep the engine running until I finish clearing the house. If I don't return in two minutes, or something looks suspicious, get out of here and call for help." He handed Asia his cell phone.

For once, she didn't comment, and her serious expression said she understood. Asia slid behind the wheel and locked the doors.

Slade headed toward the house, Glock at the ready. He inspected the ground for footprints or tracks. Nothing appeared out of place, and there were no signs of trespassing on the grounds.

No other buildings were on the property, and someone had decorated the thick line of trees with colorful Christmas lights and ornaments. Oliver hadn't provided details on the homeowners and Slade didn't question his boss. Anything was better than taking Asia to jail.

He completed his external surveillance at the rear of the ranch-style house, climbed the four wooden steps and unlocked the back door. He entered the premises through the eat-in kitchen and shut the door, warding off the increased windchill.

A square dining table was pushed against the wall separating the kitchen and living room. Slade continued into the living area, where a blue-flowered sofa and an oval coffee table took up most of the confined space. The large picture window faced the front of the house and the thick drapes were closed. He pulled back the curtains, ensuring no one hid behind them, and caught sight of Asia waiting in the car, engine running. Their eyes met before he turned and resumed his trek into the hallway and bedrooms. He moved through the rooms, checking under the beds and inside each closet.

When he reached the bathroom, he paused at the door. A polka-dot shower curtain hung over the claw-foot tub. In a swift motion, he brushed back the curtain, revealing an empty space. Finally, Slade hastened down the basement steps into a windowless, rectangular cement room, vacant except for an aged washer, dryer, furnace and water heater.

With a sigh of relief, he hurried up to the main level and out the front door.

He gave Asia a thumbs-up sign, and she unlocked the doors then shut off the engine. He helped her from the car. "All clear."

"Good to know." She wrapped herself in a hug, looking youthful and downright adorable in her black hoodie with her hair pulled into a high ponytail. Yet he didn't miss the shadows under her eyes. "Brrr. It's freezing."

Slade shoved his hands into his coat pockets to keep from pulling her into his arms. "Wearing your coat would help." He gestured to the red winter jacket she held.

The rumble of an engine caught his attention, and he spun to see a pickup barreling toward them.

Asia grasped his arm. "Who's that?"

"Beardly." Slade pinned her with a no-nonsense stare. "Listen, he's only here to ask about what you remember. It's important that you're honest with him."

"As opposed to the story I concocted for you?" She gave him a wry smile that both irked and humored Slade. The woman had a strange effect on him.

"Go on inside." Slade gestured toward the house, and she complied, shutting the door behind her.

Slade stood at the bottom of the porch steps while Beardly parked next to the unmarked sedan and killed the engine.

The man took his time exiting the vehicle, and Slade considered heading into the house. At last, Beardly climbed out, carrying a cardboard drink carrier. "Perfect timing," he announced in his unmistakable grating voice.

"Yeah, we just arrived."

"Thought you might need a pick-me-up after your adventurous night." Beardly wore his patrol-issued winter coat and a lopsided grin.

Trey's pickup rumbled onto the property, and he parked beside Beardly's vehicle.

The approach had Beardly spinning on his heel. "I didn't realize your brother would be here." He glanced down at the cardboard drink carrier with three cups.

"No worries. Trey and Magnum don't like coffee."

"Alrighty." But the man's grin had evaporated.

Slade held the door open. "Thanks for bringing the java. There's not enough caffeine in the world to recoup a lost night's sleep."

Beardly chuckled and stepped into the house. "I hear that."

Trey and his Belgian Malinois Magnum hurried over. "Nice ride, bro." Trey gestured toward the nondescript four-door blue sedan.

"Oliver suggested it for anonymity," Slade said.

His brother laughed. "You might as well get used to cars like that. They'll never issue you another new Charger."

Slade sighed at his sibling's gift for stating the obvious. "I'll probably end up with a twenty-year-old relic."

Trey snickered and stepped into the house with Slade trailing behind. Sunlight beamed through the large picture window where four adults and a seventy-pound dog overcrowded the space. Asia wore her coat and shrank into the cushions at the far right side of the sofa. Her vulnerability had Slade nearly hopping over the oval table to sit next to her. Trey's quirked eyebrow said the move wasn't exactly stealthy.

Beardly placed the cardboard drink carrier on the table, and the delicious aroma of coffee wafted upward. "I wasn't sure what everyone would want, so I got black coffees." He reached into his coat pocket, withdrawing several packets of sugar and little plastic containers of creamer, tossing them next to the cups.

"Thank you," Asia replied.

"Help yourselves. I'll grab chairs from the dining room." Beardly shuffled out and returned with two chairs, setting them opposite the sofa. Magnum lay next to Asia and lifted his large triangular head, emitting a low growl.

"Hey, pooch," Beardly said warily.

"Mags," Trey warned.

The dog quieted, but his eyes followed Beardly.

"This place is freezing." Trey studied the thermostat on the wall. "No wonder. It's only forty degrees."

"Pilot light must be out." Slade stood.

"Don't get up—I'll check," Beardly offered.

"Furnace is in the basement." Slade pointed to the far end of the kitchen.

"Be right back." Beardly disappeared down the steps.

Trey dropped onto the chair closer to the door, and Magnum moved to his side. "I went through the hospital surveillance video and found something interesting."

Slade removed the coffees from the carrier and passed one to Asia. "Do share."

"Thanks." She emptied three sugar packets into her cup.

"Later," Trey mumbled as Beardly returned.

"Yep, got the pilot relit. Should heat up quick." Beardly slid into the remaining chair, slipping off his coat. He snatched a creamer packet and dumped it into the cup in front of him, then leaned back, crossing one leg over his knee. "Heard you all had quite the scare last night. I stopped by to check on Trooper Fisher. She's got a nasty headache but no serious injuries. Said she'd be released today."

Though the man's words weren't rude or accusatory, Fisher's injury on Slade's watch stung his pride. He made a mental note to stop and visit her. "I'm grateful the masked gorilla attacker didn't kill her. The coward bolted wearing the disguise. I'm hopeful we can find a way to identify him or the vehicle off the hospital garage security cameras."

Beardly raised an eyebrow and jutted his chin. "Maybe getting a second pair of eyes on the recording would be beneficial."

Defensiveness rose and perched on Slade's shoulders. The desire to propel himself with caffeine overrode his retort, and he allowed the warm liquid to revive his brain.

Beardly continued, "No shame. You'd had a horrible night. Could've missed something inadvertently."

Slade took another sip and worked to keep his voice even. "I couldn't agree more."

"Yeah, I'm going through the recording again." Trey's tone prevented Slade from probing for more information. "Magnum and I'll monitor the perimeter while you all talk." He grabbed the dog's leash and headed out the door.

Beardly took a sip of his coffee, and something akin to annoyance passed over his face. He addressed Asia. "You've got a team of gifted troopers working your case, Mrs. Stratton."

"I guess." She fidgeted with her cup.

"It's been a long time. I'm not sure if you remember me." The investigator leaned forward.

"I do. From the funeral," Asia replied, meeting Slade's eyes.

Had it been almost a year since Zander's funeral?

He nodded and glanced down. "Yes, ma'am. I'm sorry for your loss."

"Thank you," Asia mumbled, focused on her hands.

"I need to take your statement. Formalities, since the lab results will tell us plenty." Beardly reached into his jacket and produced a small notepad and pen.

Slade remained neutral but inwardly cringed.

"Since you've had the opportunity to process everything, do you remember more? How did you end up in the trailer with Nevil Quenten?"

"Not a thing."

Beardly made a note. "What about the drugs?"

"There was nothing found in her system besides the scopolamine," Slade said, then gave himself a mental slap for jumping into the conversation.

Beardly tilted his head, narrowing his beady blue eyes. "Scopolamine. No kidding? I didn't know that was detectable under a normal tox screen."

How much had Oliver told him? "I had a hunch and asked the lab to run the tests."

"Quick results. You must have great connections." The man grinned. "Have you considered moving to Investigations? You have a knack for it."

Was the guy for real? "Not my style. I prefer working the road."

The detective chuckled. "I get that."

Slade lowered his defenses. Had he misjudged Beardly?

"Some days I miss being just a trooper, especially when my phone's gone off ten times in the middle of the night for an active case."

The snide remark reestablished Slade's defensiveness, though Beardly appeared oblivious to the dig. "Well, let's start at the beginning."

Asia inhaled and provided the same recap of the evening she'd told Slade.

Beardly addressed him. "What were you doing way out there?"

"I received a text."

The man snapped his fingers. "Oh yes, Oliver told me that."

Slade weighed his words. "The message was a cry for help, along with a screenshot of her location."

"Hmm." Beardly sipped his coffee as uneasiness oozed between them. The evidence combined with his suppositions painted Asia with motive and opportunity.

"I never sent the message," Asia blurted.

Beardly's head snapped up. "It came from your phone though."

"Anyone could've sent it," she rebutted.

"Too many puzzling pieces." Beardly made notes. "Hmm. Ma'am, are you aware cocaine was found in your purse at the trailer?"

Slade swallowed.

"I am, but it's not mine."

Beardly grabbed his coffee and set down the notepad. "Can I take off the investigator hat for a moment?"

A pause hung in the air.

"Any jury would understand you killing Quenten. I sympathize with you. The guy dragged Zander into a life of crime."

Asia remained silent. Wise.

"Considering your husband's history, it'd be logical if you'd taken up using to cope with your grief. Admitting your addiction and opting for rehab might convince the judge to be more lenient—"

Asia bolted upright. "I'm not an addict! I've never used drugs."

Beardly shrugged, and his neck all but disappeared.

What was the guy trying to do? Slade recalled his father's saying about holding your enemies close. "Opiates would've shown up on the tox screen."

"Right, right. I forgot about that. Forgive me, Mrs. Stratton. I didn't mean to offend you." Beardly's watch beeped. "Crazy. One thing after the other today." He slapped his knees. "Well, I think I have what I need. I'll be in touch once we get the gunshot residue results."

"I'll walk you out." Slade jumped up, eager for the man to leave.

When they'd stepped outside the door, Beardly paused and lowered his voice. "Be careful with that one. I'd hate to think she has it out for you. I mean, she'd made it clear with the higher-ups that she blamed you for her man's murder." He leaned closer. "You don't imagine she *lured* you out there to kill you after she took care of Quenten?"

A chill inched up Slade's neck. Every logical argument he might offer flew out of his brain, leaving him with a complete void. He cleared his throat. "She's angry, yes, but she's no vigilante."

Beardly sighed. "Yeah, I s'pose you're right. That would've taken a lot of premeditation on her part. It's just... I keep thinking about the way she took off after Zander's funeral, and out of nowhere she returns to Newman Valley. Then we find Quenten dead? Her hate would have to be off the charts to want to kill you." Beardly planted a beefy hand on Slade's shoulder and he struggled not to smack it off. "Hey, man, no one blames you. You did the right thing. Zander had it coming."

There had to be a way to end this conversation. As if sensing his discomfort, Trey and Magnum approached, and the dog emitted another throaty growl. *"Nein,"* Trey admonished, using German commands. "Finished?"

"Definitely." Beardly moved toward his truck. "I'd better get to the office and do real investigative work instead of churning nonsense around my old brain. I'll be in touch."

Slade followed his brother into the house and closed the door. The rumble of Beardly's engine faded off the property.

"You did great, Asia."

She shrugged. "I need to use the restroom."

Trey cleared his throat and pressed his lips into a thin line, waving Slade closer to the door.

"Magnum's not a fan of Beardly." Slade reached down to pat the dog's head.

"He's a great judge of character. I don't like that guy." Trey glanced toward the bathroom and lowered his voice. "There's something you should know."

Had the lab in Omaha found additional evidence already?

"Kramer contacted Oliver."

Slade groaned. "Great. Because Asia's got a connection to law enforcement."

District Attorney Grayson Kramer had exploited Zander's atrocities and murder for his political platform, spreading his "no one's above the law" zero-tolerance policy.

Trey nodded. "He's super interested in Asia's case and pushing for an arrest. Rumor is he's demanding a press conference later today to name her as a suspect."

Slade's stomach twisted into a knot. "He can't do that! The lab hasn't finished processing the evidence yet."

"No, but Kramer's influencing that process too."

Desperation to help Asia skyrocketed into urgency.

"One more thing," Trey said. "Callista caught me in the office this morning."

This day was improving by the second. Sergeant Oliver's inherited secretary, Callista Neff, was famous for faking empathy while stirring the pot and gathering information from her unsuspecting victims. "Did you escape unscathed?"

Trey snorted. "I kept her talking so she wouldn't squeeze anything out of me."

"And?"

"She said Beardly's a frequent visitor to Oliver. He's concerned about your personal relationship with Asia. Worried it'll skew your objectivity."

"Oliver's expressed the same opinion." Slade wanted to

refute the matter, but the same fear had tumbled around his brain all morning. He was too close, and in too deep, to stop now. He'd see Asia's case through, one way or the other. "Trey, I'd never risk your life or career. I promise, if things don't go well—"

Trey slapped Slade's back. "I've got your six, bro."

He exhaled relief at Trey's cop slang promising Slade could count on his brother. "I have to help her. If I had an inkling she was guilty, I'd be the first to say so. She's innocent. There's no way she murdered Quenten."

Trey shoved his hands into his pockets. "I trust your judgment, but without evidence—"

The sound of running water and the opening of the bathroom door halted the discussion. Asia returned and paused by the kitchen entrance. "Wow, that smell is awful. Think there are any scented candles around here?" She moved toward the cabinets and pulled several open before producing a large decorative candle encased in glass. Tugging open a drawer, she withdrew an old silver Zippo lighter. "These are the best. You don't burn your finger holding down the button while trying to light a candle."

Slade moved closer to her and inhaled the stench of rotten eggs. The scent grew worse as he neared the gas stove. He met Trey's eyes. "Do you smell that?"

"Gas!" Trey snatched Magnum's leash and yanked open the back door.

Slade grabbed Asia's arm, causing her to knock the glass container off the counter. He smacked the lighter out of her other hand, and it toppled to the linoleum, still aflame.

"Slade, let go!"

He ignored her demand and yanked her outside.

The group aimed for the road, their feet hammering the frozen ground. Asia slipped on an icy patch, but Slade caught her before she fell. Hefting her into his arms, he lunged for safety.

They reached the gravel just as the house exploded into flames.

FIVE

A frigid breeze and the rancid stench of smoke blew over Asia where she lay sprawled on the icy ground beside Slade. Her ears rang from the blast, a great reminder she was alive.

"Are you okay?" Trey and Magnum rushed to them.

Asia scrambled to her feet, grasping Slade's hand. "Yes, I think so." She brushed the snow off her hoodie and pants. "What just happened?"

"Natural gas explosion." Slade withdrew his phone and requested emergency assistance before shifting closer to Trey. The men spoke in hushed tones, their voices fading into the background of the raging fire.

Asia stood rooted in place, her gaze transfixed on the small house consumed by orange-and-red flames stretching up to the cloudless sky—a horrific contrast to the holiday-card-worthy property. She spotted a section of the sofa's blue floral print amid the wood and debris burying the sedan and Trey's pickup. The full realization of their near demise slammed into her chest, and she gasped, hand over her mouth to keep from crying out.

Slade moved to her side and draped his coat over her shoulders. "Help's on the way."

"We could've been killed," she whispered.

"But we weren't. If you hadn't smelled the gas—" The growl of an approaching truck interrupted him.

Detective Beardly's vehicle.

"Well, well, look who returned just in time?" Trey pulled Magnum closer.

"Don't jump to conclusions. We don't know what caused the gas leak," Slade said. "And the last thing we need is to accuse him right now."

She couldn't agree more. Upsetting the man in charge of her investigation would be idiotic. Still…was Trey implying Beardly tried to kill them?

Beardly parked his pickup a few feet away, jumped from the vehicle and jogged toward them.

He thrust a blanket around Asia's shoulders, and she reluctantly tugged it tighter. "Thank you."

"Wow. Are you all right?" He didn't wait for their response. "I was headed north when I saw the flames. Man, I thought you all were dead."

"Yeah, it's a good thing you left when you did," Trey said, suspicion in his tone.

"No kidding!"

"Did you notice anything unusual when you went down to check the pilot light?" Trey pressed.

Beardly worked his jaw. "I'm not sure I like your implication, Trooper. If I had seen something wrong, I would've said so." His beady eyes homed in on Trey.

"No one's accusing you. I didn't smell the gas when I cleared the house before you all arrived either," Slade intervened, stepping between the men.

That seemed to pacify Beardly. "Let's get into my truck. It's too cold for us to be having this conversation out here."

"That's a great idea. We don't want to add anything worse to this day," Asia said, reaching for Trey's arm. He gave her a knowing look.

If Beardly was responsible for the explosion, Asia had one more enemy—and things had just gotten very complicated.

"That's two vehicles in two days." Oliver's complaint sounded more like a whine than a rebuke.

Slade grimaced. "In all fairness, I wasn't in either of them at the time of their destruction, so technically it's not my fault."

Oliver quirked a brow. "Doubtful the colonel will view it that way."

Emergency personnel flooded the property, while firefighters worked to put out the flames.

Eager to get Asia to a safe place, Slade proposed, "Unless you need us to stick around, I'd like to take off."

"And go where?" Oliver emphasized his remark by gesturing toward the charred remains of the country home. "I don't have a surplus of safe houses, Jackson."

Slade glanced down, building the courage to make his request. Oliver's answer would be irrelevant because he and Trey had already determined to follow through with the plan. "I need to move her to safety."

"This was a safe place," Oliver groused, shaking his head. "What am I going to tell my brother?"

"This was his home?" Slade stared at the aftermath with new regret.

Oliver sighed. "He and his wife are snowbirds. Forget about it. That's my problem, not yours."

Slade shoved his hands into his coat pockets. "Sir, who knew we'd be here?"

"Besides me?"

Slade nodded.

"You, Trey and Beardly."

"Thing is, when we arrived, I cleared the premises and

found nothing out of the ordinary. I never smelled the gas, even in the basement." Slade explained how Beardly had offered to check the pilot light then left before the explosion.

"Trooper Jackson, I hope you're not implying what I think you are."

"His departure was convenient."

"And how would he guarantee the timing of the blast?" Oliver's tone was incredulous.

Slade broached the allegation delicately, Trey's suppositions hovering in his mind. "He could've timed a detonator to create a spark and set his watch alarm to give him an opportunity to leave before it exploded."

"For your sake, I'd keep that suspicion to yourself until we have a viable explanation from the fire marshal for the explosion. It also could've been coincidental and happened while Beardly was still in the house."

"With all due respect, I don't believe in coincidence."

"With no evidence, your accusation will make Beardly an instant enemy. And for Asia's sake, that would be unwise," Oliver warned.

"Noted. I'm just laying out the facts."

"Hmm." Oliver looked past Slade to where Beardly stood talking to the fire department battalion chief. A look Slade couldn't read passed over the man's face.

"Sir, I respectfully request to move Asia to an undisclosed location."

Oliver snapped his neck so fast, Slade wondered if he'd give himself whiplash. "You want to hide her?"

"The woman's life has been in nonstop danger. I'll keep in touch and provide regular updates. But I prefer only Trey and I know the exact locale." Slade held his breath. The audacious request might offend Oliver, but Slade prayed he'd recognized the urgency.

Oliver glanced down and shook his head. "I won't sign off on anything official—"

"Understood."

"You're also running out of time. Kramer's pushing for an arrest."

Slade gritted his teeth. "I've got forty-eight hours before the Omaha lab finishes processing the evidence." And either confirmed or refuted Asia's part in Quenten's death.

"You'd best make good use of them."

"What about Beardly?" Slade jerked his head toward the investigator still chatting it up with the battalion chief.

"Last time I checked, he reports to me, not you." Oliver's abrupt answer put Slade in his place. "I'm giving you a lot of leeway here. Don't make a fool of me, Jackson."

"I won't, sir."

"And I'm not issuing you another department vehicle. However, I'll allow you to drive Beardly's pickup into town, get your own and then drop his off at the office. He'll ride back with me."

"Thank you."

"Try not to destroy this truck."

"Copy that." A grin tugged at Slade's lips, and he forced it down.

"You'd better go while Beardly's occupied with the fire chief."

Slade nodded appreciation and sprinted to the truck where Asia waited. Trey stood guard beside her door. "Let's go."

"He agreed?" Trey assisted Magnum into the back seat of the crew cab. "Dog, you need a diet."

"He didn't say no," Slade clarified, climbing in.

"What's going on?" Asia's query weighed heavy with exhaustion.

"Trust us," Trey said.

Two words that Asia would accept from his sibling, but not him. She didn't persist in her questioning, and no one spoke the remainder of the ride. Each was lost in their own thoughts.

When they reached Trey's brick house two miles outside Newman Valley, he ran inside and returned with a bag of essentials for himself and Magnum, along with his personal laptop. He loaded the dog into his rusted King Cab dually pickup. With a wave, he signaled the go-ahead to their plan. He would follow them to return Beardly's vehicle. Then they'd continue the rest of the commute together.

"Can't believe he still drives that old thing," Asia said.

"Hey, I'll have you know older vehicles are easier to work on, and sometimes more reliable."

She shrugged. "Why did Trey need his own laptop?"

"We're eliminating any traceable electronics. I promise to give you all the details once we get to the house."

They dropped off Beardly's vehicle, and while Trey delivered the keys to the receptionist, Slade and Asia transferred to Trey's truck.

"You can sit in the front," Slade offered.

Asia slid next to Magnum. "That's okay. I don't mind riding in the back."

"I can move him into his kennel if you prefer," Trey said, returning to them.

"No, he's fine." She clicked her seat belt into place. "I love dogs, and Magnum's a handsome boy."

The dog panted with an expression resembling a smile.

"Yeah, and he knows it." Trey reversed out of the parking lot.

"You didn't like that old Beardly either, did you?" Asia cooed from the back seat.

Trey shot Slade an I-told-you-so smirk. He replied with

an eye roll and swiveled to face her. "Magnum's intelligent, but he doesn't speak."

"Sure he does, in his own way." She grinned, drawing attention to her full lips.

Slade's heart did a strange flip. He needed sleep. Bad.

Ten minutes later, Asia sat beside Slade in his classic muscle car. He'd prized and meticulously maintained the hot rod since high school, and Asia's presence brought back too many wonderful memories, like drive-in movies and cruising Main Street on Saturday nights.

Slade cranked the ignition, breathing life into the engine that he and Trey had rebuilt, to silence the internal movie reel playing in his memory. "We have to let Big Sally warm up before we take off."

Asia chuckled. "You still call this beast Big Sally?"

He grinned at the hot rod's nickname. "Shh, you'll hurt her feelings," he joked.

She rolled her eyes. "I can't believe you're willing to drive your baby on these roads in the dead of winter."

"This is an emergency, and she has no traceable electronics."

"Ah, smart move."

"You're in professional hands, Mrs. Stratton."

"I appreciate that, and although I love a good mystery, my perspective has changed since becoming the main character in this one. So I'd like a little more information about our next steps."

Slade palmed the steering wheel. "Fair enough."

"Let's start with where Trey went."

"He'll take a shorter route to the house, ensuring he arrives before us. Once he's cleared the property, he'll send a text and we'll head that way. Oh, and I asked him to grab food."

"Now you have my full attention. Why didn't you mention that earlier?" Her stomach growled, and Asia's cheeks flushed red.

Slade chuckled. "I'm hungry too."

"You guys have thought this plan through."

"We're no amateurs." He grinned and shifted into Drive. Slade's home was a mile from the county highway, and he couldn't wait to open the engine on the almost vacant road.

"Where's our final destination?"

"About twenty minutes from here in Meadow Hills. Faster if we don't hit the train near Monroe."

She shrugged. "Neither town sounds familiar, but I'm a homebody. Rarely go outside of Newman Valley. As long as I'm protected from potential killers, I guess location doesn't matter."

"You'll be safe."

Asia turned on the radio, but the massive engine drowned out the music and she switched it off. "Are you speeding?"

"I'm a trained professional." Slade glanced down at the speedometer. Okay, he was speeding a little. He lightened the pressure on the accelerator. "Sally's such a brute, it feels like we're going faster than we are."

"If you say so."

Slade concentrated on the highway's yellow lines, avoiding the persistent questions tumbling in his brain. No matter how hard he forced his thoughts in other directions, Beardly's insinuation hovered like a pesky fly.

He'd only worsen the fractured relationship with Asia by vocalizing his queries. Instead, he fought to rationalize the conversation with the detective or at least shove it away.

After months of he and Asia not speaking to one another—or rather, her refusing to speak to him—they'd returned to a place of cordial communication. Her barrier of disdain had shifted, giving him hope of peace between them.

A false peace? He glanced over at the pretty brunette. She stared out the passenger window, providing a clear view of the bandaged wound on the back of her head. It was improbable that her injuries were self-inflicted, but faking memory loss wasn't out of the question. Surely she'd have made a mistake and slipped up in her story if that was the case. He'd considered amnesia defenses pure fallacy used only in spy novels, but desperation was a rule changer.

His gaze returned to the rural landscape, and the single doubt he'd avoided landed smack-dab in front of him. Taunting him. Had Asia lured him to that trailer to die? Beardly's comment trailed on the heels of the uncertainty. *Her hate would have to be off the charts to want to kill you.*

Slade swallowed and worked his hands over the steering wheel. He'd left his ex-partner an open target for Quenten's men and made Asia a widow. That provided her with motive.

Asia's grief had exploded into fury, and she'd told anyone who'd listen to her that she blamed Slade. But murder? He shook his head, arguing with the one-sided dialogue. No, even in her anger, Asia was incapable of such evil.

His time would be better spent identifying whoever else had been in the trailer with her. And worst-case scenario, find another way to get her out of this situation. Failure meant an innocent woman would go to prison. Not an option.

He sat up straighter and cranked the heater and radio, drowning out his internal deliberation.

Asia leaned over and turned off the radio again. "Do you think Quenten's men killed him over that card?"

"Anything is possible."

"What am I going to do?"

Slade bit the inside of his cheek and prayed for a stroke of brilliance. "Let's take it all one step at a time." Well, that was a lame reply.

She pivoted to face him. "In case you haven't noticed, I'm sort of on a deadline. I can't wait for the slow wheels of justice to roll in my situation."

"Interfering could make things worse. If we uncover anything that will help you, we'll have to contact Beardly." *Internal policy manual strikes again.*

"He's the one who thinks I'm guilty." The bite in her tone melted into a quiver. "I'm no killer."

Slade sighed. He had an irrefutable way of upsetting her. "No one thinks—"

"Yes, they do." She turned away.

"If you can't remember the past two days, how can you be sure?" Warmth radiated up his cheeks. He'd spoken his doubt. He had to stop talking. Slade rubbed the back of his neck. "What I meant was, until we find the missing pieces, we have to remain transparent. Think through all the possibilities."

She huffed. "Do you ever drift from being the perfect rule follower?"

"Have I arrested you yet? I've more than proven I can go outside the rules."

The death glare Asia shot him could've smoked a ham. "Tell me again how no one thinks I'm guilty."

"Hear me out. Maybe establishing a reason for *why* you had to shoot Quenten makes more sense." He focused again on the road. What he'd give to pull a heroic action movie rescue for her. They'd run far away from this mess and then return with the evidence to exonerate her, right before the credits spun.

But this was real life. They wouldn't hide, and he couldn't

let her go free if she was guilty. Friend or not, she'd be incarcerated. The law was blind to gray areas like friendship. If only his heart were blind to Asia and agreed with his logic.

His gaze drifted to her. "Hey, I shouldn't have—"

The roar of an engine snagged his attention.

A truck grille filled his rearview mirror.

Before Slade processed the visual, a jolt to the rear end sent Big Sally swerving.

He recovered from the fishtail and regained control. The pursuer advanced again and made impact a second time, thrusting them forward. Confusion collided with reality at the volatile attack.

"If they run us off the road, we're dead!" Asia's statement of the obvious increased Slade's tension.

He accelerated, hoping to outrun the pursuers, but the truck stayed close behind.

Another slam propelled them sideways.

Slade jerked the wheel, and his response had the car deviating through the ice-covered median as he battled the velocity forcing them out of control. He corrected the move, and they bounced across the highway into the southbound lanes. Thankfully, there was no oncoming traffic on the rural road.

His grip tightened on the steering wheel as he moved them back to his lane. He tapped the brakes. The pedal slammed against the floorboard.

Heart jackhammering against his ribs, Slade pumped the brakes, but the car seemed to have a mind of its own and continued to speed up.

Asia screamed and he jerked the wheel, avoiding a mile marker pole by inches. *Dear God.* His two-word prayer held the desperate plea for rescue and survival.

"I don't have brakes!" He slammed his foot repeatedly against the pedal, but it was useless.

"Slade, do something!"

But he couldn't stop. The truck pursued them.

Desperate, Slade yanked the wheel. The overcorrection sent the car careening into the ditch.

"Hang on!" In terrifying slow motion, dark shapes blurred outside the window.

He turned, meeting Asia's terror-filled expression.

Big Sally landed with a slam on the driver's side, went airborne, then smashed down again. The impact shook every part of his body. Each horrific, recurring tug of gravity imprisoned them like riders on a nightmare amusement park ride.

He squeezed his eyes shut, willing the vehicle to yield. Each repeated lurch rattled the interior of the car, stealing his breath. He couldn't yell. Couldn't breathe.

Asia's shrieks melded with the screeching metal and shattering glass as the hot rod rolled.

Finally, the acrobatics stopped, and they landed with a last bounce on the tires. Sally's broken engine hissed.

Slade gasped and stretched across to Asia, ignoring the excruciating pain in his arm until he touched flesh. "Asia, staydow—!" he slurred. "Juss—gedown!" Why couldn't he talk?

Frustrated, he reached for his gun. The movement sent electric shocks up his left arm, which hung limp at his side. Gritting his teeth, he grappled in clumsy, awkward slaps.

At last his fingers wrapped around the metal and he tugged the Glock free from his hip holster. A thick substance oozed over his eye, blurring his vision. Weapon in hand, he swiped, coating his wrist in blood.

"Are they—" came Asia's voice.

"Shh!" he hissed, grateful she was alive and praying she kept quiet.

Slade wiped at his face again while the drumming in his brain pulsated behind his eyes.

Doors slammed.

His whole body vibrated from the rushing river of adrenaline. Slade searched where the side mirrors had once hung. Only broken pieces remained. He reverted his gaze to the rearview mirror, watching in the fragmented slivers.

Two figures approached, their footsteps drawing closer.

Asia dug her fingernails into the seat cushion, grounding herself as she worked to calm her breathing. Shards of glass from her window pricked her hand and arm. Smoke billowed from the hood.

She jerked to look at Slade. He mouthed "Get down," pointed to the mirror, then gestured to the floorboards. Was he trying to hide her? Or did he see something she couldn't? A crimson stream colored the left side of his face near his hairline. There'd be worse damage than that if the men got to them.

She nodded, released her seat belt and did her best to scoot down.

"Kill the cop," a man's voice ordered.

Snow crunched outside, and she sucked in a breath.

Slade stretched across her and lifted his gun, watching in the rearview mirror. She twisted around, searching for the men. Two large shadows stood near the trunk but remained at a safe distance.

"Why aren't you shooting at them?" she hissed.

He winced and shifted, giving Asia a glimpse of his left arm, limp in his lap. She held out her hand. "You're hurt. Give me your gun."

Slade shook his head.

"Don't be stupid. You can't take us both on. Send out the

woman. She's not worth dying for. Cooperate and I might let you live," a man called.

Asia slid upward, peering over the seat's headrest. The men had flanked the car, surrounding them from behind. If he shot one, the other had opportunity to fire.

"Not a chance," Slade responded.

"I only want to ask her a question."

"Then why try to kill us a hundred different ways?" He slouched low in the seat, keeping his gun at the ready, but his hand shook. He scowled, swiped at his forehead and adjusted slightly, no doubt trying to get a better angle for the shot.

"You're wasting your time. One way or the other, we will take her. And we'll eliminate any obstacles. You're no hero. Your pathetic driving proved that." The man roared with laughter.

"You have my word. I won't kill her. I only want what she's holding for me," the other man responded.

"What's he talking about? I don't have anything!" Frustration tightened Asia's stomach, and she fisted her hands.

Slade met her eyes. Was that doubt written in the copper flecks? "Fine. Put your gun down, and she'll exit the vehicle."

Asia bolted upright in the seat. "Are you out of your mind?"

Slade tilted his head, annoyance etched in his expression. No, he was bluffing. Unless he pivoted and secured his target, it'd be impossible for him to take out both taunting criminals.

"Give me the gun," she repeated.

"When I tell you to, throw open your door and get down," Slade ordered.

Asia twisted and peered over the seat where the back window had once been. "I've got a direct hit from here."

"If I do as you ask, how do I know you won't open fire?" the man interrupted, his voice drawing closer.

"You don't," Slade answered.

"Then we're at an impasse. I'm done negotiating. Send her out or I'll kill you and take her."

Asia swallowed hard. Did Big Sally still work? Why wasn't Slade driving away? Yet she remained in their silent standoff, waiting for instruction.

Slade reached into his pocket, wincing with the movement, and dropped his cell phone into her hand. "Call for help." He twisted around and focused on his side of the car.

Shaking violently, her fingers bounced across the numbers until she entered 9-1-1. She tightened her grip, sliding her thumb over the screen and praying she connected with the green icon initiating the call.

Slade fired out of his broken window. Asia jerked to look at him.

"Nine-one-one. What's your emergency?" the operator's tinny voice asked from her hand.

She glanced down.

Footsteps pounded behind her and she turned, cringing at the shadow that hovered beside her.

"Help! Send help to—"

A smack to the side of her head sent the phone flying into the windshield with a sickening thud. It slid off the dashboard and out Slade's window, exhausting any last hope of rescue.

"Help!" she repeated. Could the operator hear her? She twisted around and came nose to barrel with the gun pointed in her window. Her gaze traveled upward, but the massive arm and torso blocked the light. The man was enormous.

"Drop your gun and tell your friend to get out of the car," the brute beside Slade ordered.

Asia gasped at the gun barrel pointed at his temple.

"You'll have to kill me first." Slade didn't flinch, but worry swam in his golden irises.

"That can be arranged," the man countered.

"Don't hurt him. I'll do what you want." Asia focused on Slade and gripped the door handle, pushing it open.

"Asia, no!" Slade hollered.

"Wise move," the man beside her commented, shifting over, gun never wavering.

She climbed out of the destroyed automobile. Keeping close to the door, she glanced up from the wall of a chest until she met the dark eyes and hostile scowl of her guard.

Please, Lord, help me.

He took a step backward, giving her full view of him, but maintained a steady aim of his weapon. The man's murderous glare narrowed, and his massive frame eclipsed the sunlight. Scraggly black hair resembled an ill-fitting toupee, and an unkempt beard partially covered his face.

"Where's the card?" he growled, baring his yellowed teeth.

"I...I...don't—" Her jaw chattered as adrenaline flooded her system. She surveyed the car. Doubtful it was drivable.

The man advanced in a slow, measured maneuver. She took a grapevine step to the side—the two moving in a strange waltz of avoidance—until she ran out of the car and stumbled backward. She gripped the car's bumper and righted herself, catching movement in her peripheral.

"Wait! Let Slade go. Then I'll tell you," Asia negotiated.

"No can do, sweetheart," the man guarding Slade said.

"Then kill us both, and you'll have nothing." Asia lifted her chin and squared her shoulders.

"Get out," the other man said.

She glanced over, feeling a hint of relief at the sight of the driver's door opening with a loud screeching complaint. Slade edged from the car. Her heart ached at the way he held his arm—likely dislocated or broken—against his side, and his head wound continued to bleed.

Slade's assailant shoved him around to the front of the vehicle. The men separated them. Divide and conquer.

If she didn't fight back, they'd both be dead.

Every self-defense skill she'd ever learned escaped her memory. What should she do?

The mountain of a man covering her closed the short distance between them. Asia turned so that the car bumper touched her left leg and she faced her attacker. The shift blocked her view of Slade.

"There, you've seen he's still alive. Now tell me." The man reached to grab her.

Asia ducked, dodging his mammoth grip and groping fingers.

"If I do as you say, will you leave us alone?" she asked, again backing away from him.

"Remember, Asia, where the head goes, the body follows," Slade hollered.

"Shut up," the other man barked.

Slade's words trickled into her brain. He knew she didn't have a clue where the card was, so what did he mean?

"Sometimes you have to get personal," Slade said.

She caught a glimpse as his guardian drove a fist into Slade's stomach, the appalling thud traveling to her ears. "Keep your mouth shut, or I'll put a bullet in your empty head," he barked.

Asia studied Slade, hoping for something more.

"Where's the card?" the man standing inches from her demanded again.

She jerked to look at him and Slade's instructions connected, illuminating her memory like Christmas lights. *Where the head goes, the body follows. Get personal.* Her self-defense training returned, and Asia studied the redwood of a man hovering over her.

"Okay." She softened her voice, drawing him in. "I'll tell you," she whispered and averted her eyes, glancing down.

He leaned closer and grasped her hair, his sour breath wafting into her face, and yanked up her head. "Speak!"

When their eyes met, Asia thrust her knee upward, landing squarely on target. The man groaned and doubled over. Threading her fingers through his scraggly hair, she slammed her thigh into his nose. He slumped to the ground.

She pivoted and saw Slade jab the elbow of his good arm into his guard's nose. The man's hands rushed to his face. Slade delivered a strike to his neck, dropping him like a sack of flour. He snatched the man's pistol and Asia mimicked his gesture, grabbing the gun from the man still splayed out at her feet. Together they ran to the criminals' truck and climbed in.

Slade accelerated, spinning the tires and throwing dirt behind them as they sped back onto the highway.

Asia snapped her seat belt into place, then groaned.

"What's wrong?"

"We forgot to pick up your phone."

"That's okay. We'll grab another in town."

Asia groped around inside the vehicle and found fast-food napkins. She pressed them into Slade's hand.

"I'm sure it looks worse than it is. Head wounds bleed a lot." He applied pressure to the injury while his tone remained calm.

"What about your arm?"

Slade gave a one-shoulder shrug. "Dislocated. I'll take

care of that when we stop too. Is there any chance you recognized either of them?"

"Not at all."

Did she read disbelief or frustration in Slade's expression?

Twenty minutes later, they pulled up to a truck stop and hurried inside.

Slade excused himself and Asia stood close to the men's restroom door, despite the curious looks from passersby. A loud slam on the opposite wall of the bathroom preceded Slade's return. His arm looked normal.

"I'm scared to ask what you did to fix your arm."

"Let's just say I might consider chiropractic school when I retire."

She winced. "Maybe I'd have been better off not knowing."

"It's all good. The wall was very helpful in the relocation process." He shrugged and moved past her.

Who was this guy?

They navigated through the small store with its sparsely spaced aisles until they found the burner phones.

Slade snatched a cell from the display and a package of cinnamon gum. Asia grabbed a box of Band-Aids.

A single cashier worked the counter. With the speed of a sloth walking through molasses, she rang up the items. Slade slapped cash down. "Keep the change," he said, clearly as anxious to get out of the store as Asia.

Once they were in the truck again, Slade swiveled to face her. The depth in his caramel eyes consumed and enveloped her in a powerful grasp. "I want you to know something."

"Okay." She searched his face, placing a Band-Aid over the wound.

"You're not alone in this. I'm all in, whatever it takes. I'll fight for you."

I'll fight for you. Four words that probed the secret longing of her heart with a promise she'd longed to hear her entire life. Tears threatened, and Asia blinked them away, forcing a smile. "I don't remember if I said thank you for the clothes," she said, smoothing down the black hoodie, desperate to change the subject.

"I can't take credit. Trey did the actual purchasing. A benefit of having sisters is the ability to shop for women."

Images of the boisterous Jackson sisters embracing Asia into their family, and the night of her and Slade's senior prom, brought a bittersweet flashback. The girls had doted on her, fixing her hair and makeup. It was a wonderful evening. Sadly, it was also the last time she and Slade had been a couple. Regret slammed into her for that one pivotal moment where she wished to reverse time and choose differently.

Slade's familiar presence gave her a strange sense of comfort. Maybe she'd give him a chance to regain her trust, because at this point, who else did she have to turn to? Yet the voice in her heart shouted, *Don't trust him!*

Slade offered her a piece of gum, but she refused. He called Trey and gave him a quick recap of their adventure. "Pick us up at the deserted Mayer farm off of Highway 20." Next, he contacted Oliver. "Sarge, there've been some developments."

Asia half-heartedly listened while scouring her mind. Something familiar clawed at the back of her brain. A sound? A smell? It was as if someone had drawn a thick black curtain declaring the end of a play and eliminating her memories. She was being hunted, and her survival depended on remembering. Yet someone had injected her with an amnesiac drug. What had that person wanted her to forget?

SIX

Relief coursed through Slade as the county road opened onto Main Street's thoroughfare. Asia remained quiet after they'd ditched the criminals' truck and Trey had picked them up. The familiar wooden sign boasting Meadow Hills, Population 100 brought a smile to his lips, and he absorbed the holiday ambience exhibited in the quaint stores that paralleled the street. The display in Jack's Country Shoppe promised *the best soda fountain around*. Bright green-and-red garland draped the light poles, and an inflatable snowman brightened the picturesque town. The residents of Meadow Hills existed in nostalgia.

"Wow, it's like taking a step back in time," Asia whispered. "This place is adorable."

"Reminds me of an old 1950s' television show." Trey turned onto the street leading to the house. Tall trees bordered the sidewalk, heavy with snow.

"Definitely," Asia replied.

"Our great-aunt Velma lived here. When we were little, all of us kids would visit her in the summer. Good times," Slade said.

"What? How did I not know this about you and your family?" Asia asked.

"I'm an enigma, Stratton," he quipped.

Within minutes, Trey parked in front of the small bungalow Aunt Velma had bequeathed to Slade. "Here we are."

The place held no outstanding curb appeal, but it contained many fond childhood memories for Slade. More important, he prayed Aunt Velma's would be a safe place to hide and protect Asia.

"Give us five." Trey and Magnum exited the vehicle.

"He'll clear the house and check for gas leaks." Slade's cheeky comment fell flat. He was anxious to get inside.

"What did Trey bring for breakfast?" Asia pointed to the paper bag beside him on the seat.

His mouth watered with expectation as he recalled the town's famous Muffin Man Bakery's delectable treats. "The biggest and best cinnamon rolls in Nebraska. I promise I won't judge you for eating a whole one by yourself."

Asia grinned. "Wow, the way you make it sound, I haven't lived until I've eaten this mysterious, amazing pastry."

"They're as good as falling in love." Heat flushed his face. Where on earth had that come from?

The burner phone vibrated with Trey's well-timed text confirming the house was clear. The hundred-pound weight resting on Slade's shoulders lessened, but situational awareness kept him on high alert.

He thrust open the driver's door and scooted out, avoiding her response or eyes. He circled the hood and assisted Asia from the vehicle.

"I see you're ever the chivalrous escort."

Good, she hadn't heard his comment. Or she'd ignored him. Either was fine. "My father would slap me all the way from Iowa if he found out I'd behaved any less than a gallant gentleman." Slade grinned at the memories of his father's strong expectations on how to treat a woman.

"He would do no such thing. Pops is the sweetest man

I know, next to my daddy, of course. He'd be proud you're following in his footsteps." Asia smiled and released his hand.

The absence of her touch immediately registered.

Slade led Asia up the three cement steps braced by a black iron railing and tugged open the heavy wooden door as they entered the unassuming brick home. Trey and Magnum sat in the dining room facing the entry.

"Thought I'd have to send a search party out for you." Trey ruffled Magnum's fur.

Slade dropped the bakery bag on the table and moved to the kitchen for plates and utensils. "Patience never has been a virtue of yours, baby brother."

"Hey, I demonstrated great restraint by not eating them on the way to pick you up," Trey defended.

"I'm impressed," Asia said. "Slade says I haven't lived until I've had one of these cinnamon rolls."

"So true." Trey dug out one of the individual serving boxes and pried it open.

"Don't mind us," Slade teased.

"Sorry," Trey said over a mouthful of roll.

With a chuckle, Slade served the two remaining desserts on plates, passing one to Asia. He gestured toward the last plate, but Trey held up his fingers covered in cream-cheese frosting. "I'm good with the cardboard container."

Slade gave him his best act-like-a-gentleman glower.

"What?" Trey tilted his head, and Magnum mimicked his master.

Slade and Asia exchanged a glance and burst out laughing.

"Whatever." Trey stuffed another chunk into his mouth. "Mags and I are going to the other side of the house to keep watch." The duo disappeared down the hallway.

Slade dropped onto the seat beside Asia. "Please excuse my brother. He forgets his manners when confronted with food."

The burner cell phone rang from his pocket. Only two people had the number, Oliver and Trey.

He stood and answered the call.

"Jackson, everything okay?" Sergeant Oliver's voice boomed through the line.

Asia glanced up, no doubt able to hear the man.

Slade mouthed "Be right back" and walked to the living room, keeping his sights on her. "Yes, sir, we're at the house."

"Trey with you?"

"Affirmative."

"The fire inspector is working the scene."

"Has he found proof of an ignition source?"

"Not yet. The damage is extensive. I'll keep you posted. I called because the lab discovered a partial print on Zander's gun."

Slade's pulse increased, and he spun to look at Asia. "That's good news, right?"

Her dark eyes begged for answers.

"Might've been, except the print's too smudged to put it through AFIS without a comparable."

The federal Automated Fingerprint Identification System housed thousands of fingerprints, and obtaining information would take an eternity without another sample to compare against the smudged print. Slade shifted and lowered his voice. "That proves a third person was there that night."

"Not necessarily. Could be left over from when Zander possessed the gun."

Hope deflated like a week-old helium balloon. Slade rubbed the back of his neck, the heaviness of Asia's intense stare weighing on him. He suppressed a groan. How was he supposed to tell her any of this? "Thanks for the update. I'll be in touch soon." Slade disconnected before Oliver responded. He'd pay for that later.

He returned to the dining table, where Asia sat with her untouched cinnamon roll. Her leg bounced, and she bit her lip in an unspoken demand for data he didn't want to share.

"Let's eat." He slid into the chair next to her.

"What'd he say?"

"They're still looking for the ignition source of the fire. When we're done feasting on these, we'll brainstorm about the mysterious card and anyone else who could've been with you at that trailer. A full stomach might help you remember."

Asia frowned, and guilt washed over him for withholding information. Bad news wouldn't help. Stress would derail her more and block any new details. In reality, the scopolamine likely erased most if not all of her memory, yet a seed of optimism prevented Slade from surrendering. "Mind if I give thanks for our food?"

"Sure."

"Lord, please bless this food and give us the wisdom we need today. In Christ's name we pray."

"Amen." Asia lifted the plate, inhaling deeply. "I think the smell alone caused me to gain ten pounds."

"Get comfortable and dig in."

She gasped, one hand on her throat, the other still holding the plate.

"What's wrong?" Slade leaned forward.

Her skin paled, and her eyes widened. Though certain there wasn't anything behind him, he turned. His pulse increased at the concern etched on her beautiful face and her lack of verbal response.

Slade touched her arm and took the plate before she dropped it. "Asia? Talk to me."

She snapped her head in his direction and clutched his arm. "I remember something! We have to go to my apartment now!"

Panic rose in his chest as his gaze darted around. Had she seen someone?

"It's not safe—" He tried to ease her concern as her fingernails dug into his forearm.

"Now! I have to see something for myself."

"I think it's better if you stay here with Trey. Tell me what it is, and I'll go. We can't risk you getting hurt...or worse."

Asia stood, determination and stubbornness merged in her eyes. "No way. Whatever Zander was into, he dragged me in with him. I've earned the right to know what's going on. I *want* to know."

Did she? Because at that moment, Slade wasn't sure she understood the depth of her demand.

"Slade, it's the cinnamon!" Asia gripped the table, grounding herself against the flood of memories bursting through her mind.

His quizzical expression said the word didn't suffice as an explanation.

She sighed. "The cinnamon reminded me of the last time I talked to Zander."

"That's it?" Slade exhaled.

She glared.

"I'm sorry—continue."

"Right before you arrested Zander, he showed up late on my doorstep, begging for a second chance. He did that occasionally, but this time was different."

"How?"

"He wasn't under the influence."

Slade nodded, compassion written on his face.

Asia fidgeted with her fork. "He gave me a beautiful wooden whale figurine." She glanced down. The release of Zander's memories softened her heart with an ancient ache.

Slade placed a hand gently over hers. "Sometimes sharing the good frees you to live beyond the bad."

She met his eyes and blinked to clear the annoying tears. "When did you become such a philosopher?"

He grinned. "What can I say? I'm wise. And I say you need to eat."

Asia cut into her roll. "He said the gift was his promise to overcome his issues and make things right."

"Okay, but I'm lost on how cinnamon fits into this."

"We went for a long walk and talked into the morning. Then I baked some of those instant cinnamon rolls. I have no idea why the smell awakened that recollection, and it seems kind of insignificant. But doesn't it stand to reason that being in my home around familiar things might trigger something more?"

Slade shrugged, and skepticism oozed from him. "Scent is the closest link to memory, so I'd say it's worth a try. I'll look for the figurine and call you if I find it."

He didn't get it. Asia steeled her voice. "I'm not asking permission. I am going there to see for myself."

Resignation flickered in his eyes. "Fine, but only after you've eaten. I don't need you passing out on me."

Asia withdrew from his touch and forked a piece of the soft dough. Whatever got them moving faster. The spicy sweetness touched her lips, and she closed her eyes, savoring the blissful flavors. "That's amazing. I believe you've earned a whole new level of trust."

"With a cinnamon roll?" he joked.

"Something like that." Why had she said that? She'd never trust Slade completely again. Would she?

"Let me talk with Trey first. And I've got to change out of this shirt."

Even with blood smearing his light blue thermal, he maintained that cool exterior and meticulous appearance.

"How did you manage a car accident, an attempted kidnapping, a beatdown and a dislocated shoulder back in place without messing up your hair?"

Slade stood and tugged the stained garment over his head, revealing a short-sleeved black compression undershirt. "Great products." He tapped the top of his head.

What was she doing? She didn't have time to notice Slade's hair or anything else.

"Be right back." He disappeared into the bedroom.

A renewed motivation sent adrenaline flowing through her veins. Munching more of the dessert, Asia jumped up and paced. What was taking him so long? They needed to leave.

She scrolled her brain from the night Zander visited to everything leading up to Thursday. Nothing unusual stood out.

Finally, Slade and Trey emerged. "All right, let's find this whale."

He headed to the kitchen and waved Asia over while Trey and Magnum moved to the front door. She stuffed the rest of her roll into her mouth. "Aren't we riding with them?"

"No, Trey will go ahead of us." Slade tugged open the door and flipped on a light in the attached garage. "We're driving Aunt Velma's car." He gestured toward the vintage vehicle the size of a barge, which filled the space.

"I haven't seen one of these in ages."

"Yeah, it's a classic." He hit the button, activating the garage door.

Five minutes later, they sailed out of Meadow Hills and onto the highway.

"Let's focus on Thursday night. I've played out possible scenarios. What if the kidnapper broke in and drugged you while you were sleeping?" Slade asked.

Asia considered his words. "I suppose it's a possibility."

"Are you a heavy sleeper?"

"Zander used to say I'd doze through a tornado siren."

Slade palmed the steering wheel. "That gives us the how. Now we need the who and why."

Her chest tightened at images of a home invasion. "Do you think the person stalked me?"

"Are you still routine-driven?"

Had he forgotten everything about her? "You really have to ask that?"

He grinned. "I didn't want to assume."

"Why would anyone do that? Who hates me that much?" Asia rubbed the gooseflesh on her arms.

"My guess is you have a shared enemy."

She combed her mind. "Who?"

Slade worked his jaw as conflicted emotions warred in his expression.

"What aren't you telling me?"

After several seconds, he responded. "Zander backed himself into the middle of a war. Maybe he promised something he couldn't deliver and tried bargaining his way out."

Zander had had a gift for getting himself in too deep with everything he touched. Her thoughts returned to their last evening together and his words. *You think you've got it all under control, and before you know what hit you, a rope is around your neck dragging you under. And you realize you're no island. That your actions affect other people.*

She'd chalked the comment up to him being in over his head with debt. "What kind of war?"

Slade's Adam's apple bobbed. "Between drug cartels."

Asia gasped, hand over her mouth. Poor Zander. He must've been terrified. Unexpected compassion flowed through her.

"There's a detail I've never told you about the day we found him."

"Okay…" Asia studied him, tempted to demand he speak faster.

He worked the steering wheel and cleared his throat. "Zander…the thing is…the killers had…"

"Just say it."

He exhaled the words. "He'd been tortured, most likely to extract information."

Asia pressed her fingers against her quivering lips. Images raced in her mind, and she shoved them away, not wanting to visualize anything so horrid. "They murdered Zander because he didn't give them whatever they wanted? Or because he confessed?"

Neither answer would make her feel better, but not knowing the truth wasn't helping her situation. She needed all the evidence, no matter how upsetting.

"We believe a combination."

Asia squeezed her eyes shut.

"That tells you the caliber of people we're up against. We can't linger at your apartment. I want you secure in Meadow Hills. We need at least one evening without someone trying to kill us."

"I'll be quick." Asia prayed the memories would return and explain how she'd ended up sitting with Nevil Quenten. A shiver raced up her spine at the unwanted visual of his cold, dead stare.

When they reached her apartment complex forty minutes later, Asia spotted Trey's King Cab dually amid the cars from every decade imaginable filling the parking lot.

Competing music from several of the units blared at ridiculous decibels. The familiarity brought a measure of respite, easing the tension in her shoulders.

Slade shut off the engine and faced her. "Stay here until I've talked with Trey."

He stepped out, and his hand landed on the Glock holstered on his hip. With his back to Asia, he circled the vehicle, probably checking for anything suspicious. Truth be told, everything in this low-rent neighborhood was potentially suspicious.

He moved to Trey's truck and conversed with his brother.

Asia surveyed the area. Four buildings, each with three stories hosting ten apartments per level, were situated in a U shape around the pothole-infested parking lot. Dirty snow covered the ground between the units. An old abandoned sofa and several bicycles sagged against one building.

Less than desirable living conditions, but it was home.

Slade leaned on Trey's door, Asia in his line of sight. He focused past her in distracted attention, continuously surveying their surroundings. "You've cleared the area?"

"Yep, her apartment too. She's in for quite a shock when she sees the condition."

"Somehow I had a feeling that would happen."

"My guess is they started here before coming after you."

Slade thumped the door. "Still can't believe those goons destroyed Big Sally."

"We'll rebuild her this summer." Trey was always the optimist.

"Right. Anyway, give us about ten minutes, then call for the evidence guys. Maybe seeing her place will trigger her memories."

Trey nodded. "I'll get Magnum working once you leave."

"Who's keeping watch at the house?"

"Bro, check this out. I installed cameras." Trey lifted his laptop and showed Slade the live feed of his aunt's front step, where a cat traipsed around the porch then hopped down.

"Wow, we really do underestimate you." Slade caught a glimpse of Trey's boyish smile. Proof that even as an adult, his little brother still longed for affirmation.

"I didn't get a chance to tell you earlier, but I also analyzed the hospital security footage." Trey's computer skills rivaled his canine handling. If anyone found something to help Asia, he would.

"And…"

Trey tapped a few keys then displayed a video showing a masked man running from Asia's room and into the stairwell. He flipped to the camera, where the man bolted down the steps and through the garage door, Slade trailing. Trey again tapped the keyboard, shifting to the view of the empty garage. "The man escaped from the south wing of the hospital and entered a black SUV with no plates?"

"Yeah," Slade mumbled. "Except there's no footage of the SUV? It's like the guy disappeared."

"No one just disappears," Trey countered, spinning the device to face him. He tapped a few keys, bringing up the video again. "There." He pointed to the corner of the screen where a fly had perched.

"It's thirty degrees on a good day. There are no flies this time of year."

"Watch—the bug doesn't move," Trey said.

Slade studied the screen as the fly repeated the same circular pattern.

"Someone pulled old footage and looped the film," Trey explained.

"Who else had access to the security cameras?" Slade asked, annoyance building.

"Only those with a hospital security clearance badge, but that's irrelevant."

"What do you mean?"

"The cameras are controlled via computers. They can be remotely accessed."

"So breaking into the security office wasn't necessary," Slade concluded.

"Exactly."

"Unbelievable."

"I'll keep digging."

"Thanks." Slade ran a hand over his head.

"We'll catch him. Criminals are notoriously stupid. He'll mess up somewhere and we'll take him down then."

"I hope you're right." Because the clock was ticking, and he had no clue where to go from here.

He turned and headed back to Asia. She seemed to be staring off into space and visibly startled when he lifted the door handle. "Sorry, didn't mean to scare you."

She gripped his outstretched hand as he assisted her from the vehicle. "I was lost in thought."

"Looked like it. Trey cleared your apartment."

"So we're safe?"

"I wouldn't go that far. We've got a few minutes before the evidence techs arrive." He winced. Why had he said it that way?

Asia tilted her head, a quizzical expression crossing her face.

"Our friends from the highway apparently started here."

She quickened her pace, and he was forced to jog to keep up. "I should go first."

She ignored him, taking the lead as they trekked up the

cement stairs to the fourth floor. Though he'd never visited her, he knew which unit was hers.

Heavy bass music and the thick odor of fried food lingered in the cold afternoon air. They ascended the next three flights, then hastened across the walkway to her apartment at the end.

Asia gripped the paint-chipped iron rail and halted in front of what was left of her splintered door, hanging by one hinge. She pivoted and faced him, her jaw tight.

His heart squeezed at the sorrow tainted with anger reflected in her eyes, and words of comfort eluded him. A new resolve infused his veins. He would prove her innocence, because seeing Asia hurt nearly undid him.

"We're going to get through this."

She gave an almost imperceptible nod. "You have to love the irony here." She ducked inside.

"What's that?"

"I always lock my door, even if I run out to dump trash. That was effective."

"Someone must've seen who did this."

"No one in the complex will talk to cops," Asia replied.

He followed her through the entry. The open floor plan gave him an unobstructed view of the ransacked home. Papers, books and picture frames once displayed with love and pride lay strewn around the aged brown carpet, amid the dissected sofa cushions.

The destruction continued into the bedroom. He carefully avoided stepping on anything as he inspected the area. Her slashed mattress spewed its innards, ravaged beyond repair. The pillows had been ripped apart and the sheets and blankets lay scattered across the floor.

Slade returned to the living room, where Asia slumped against the kitchen counter. "I'm sorry—just give me a second to process this." Her outstretched arms gestured to the mess, and her voice increased an octave with each word until she was practically screeching. "Why would they do this? What did I ever do to deserve being attacked like some common criminal?"

She'd been through so much. He couldn't blame her faulty thinking, but they needed to stay within protocol. Slade spoke in an almost too calm tone. "None of this is your fault. This is a perfect example of why we have to keep the patrol apprised. It shows you're on someone's list and in danger. Don't touch anything. Let the crime investigators do their job. Every criminal messes up sometime. Let's hope they left fingerprints."

Asia shuffled past him and he trailed behind. She paused at the foot of her bed.

"Talk to me," he probed.

"No one will believe me. They'll spin it to support their assumption that I killed Nevil Quenten." She motioned to the disaster surrounding them.

"Were you fighting with someone here? Could that have happened on Thursday night?"

Asia shrugged. "I don't know."

"Take a deep breath and look around."

"I have been—"

"The desecration here testifies to a search. There's no question about their attacking us on the road. Do you think finding the whale will help you remember?"

"Who knows?"

He prayed something would click for her before they had to hand the scene over to the evidence techs. Whatever this card held, Zander had given his life for its secret, and someone else deemed it worth killing Quenten.

If they didn't find it fast, Asia was next.

* * *

Asia scanned the apartment, taking in the calamity that had befallen her home.

Slade shifted closer, invading her personal space. "I realize this threw you off, but take a minute and focus. Are you getting any flashes? Visions?"

Amusement battled with frustration. "That's not how it works. It's random, like when I smelled the cinnamon."

She squatted in front of her favorite picture. Broken glass had scratched her father's face, scarring her heart.

"Don't touch anything." Slade held her wrist, restricting her from touching the frame.

Asia jerked her hand back and rose, conflicted between falling apart and throwing a fit. "Once the evidence guys come rushing in, I'll lose complete control of my home." Irrational reasoning fueled impossibilities. *Just a few minutes to regain my footing or resign myself to my suffering.*

Slade said nothing, probably fighting his follow-the-rules self, but appreciation for his compliance comforted her. Hopelessness sucked energy from her, yet Slade's presence resuscitated her broken spirit, if only temporarily.

"Okay." His gentle tone and shadowed eyes revealed genuine concern.

No. Stay mad. It's safer. Letting go of her rage might release the dam barring her emotional breakdown.

A thorough survey of the destruction restored her anger to full throttle. She'd been invaded, and the evidence technicians would cover everything in black dust, collecting her things like specimens.

Asia moved around the bed and gasped at the sight of her grandmother's shredded quilt. Slade approached in slow, careful steps, as if he understood the solemnity of the moment. Kneeling, she started to gather the pieces of irreparable scraps.

Slade grabbed her arm. "You can't touch anything."

Tears blurred her vision. "Why?"

One word that encompassed her entire world.

One word that would exonerate her if it were truthfully answered.

She rocked on her heels, desperate to hold on to the remnants of her childhood. "I'm tired."

"I know." He reached for her, but she scooted away, resisting his touch. A flash of hurt crossed his face and his arms fell to his sides.

A wave of grief engulfed her, dragging her beneath its suffocating embrace. Why was someone out to destroy her?

"I'm so sorry, Asia."

Tears choked her, but she swallowed, unwilling to yield to them. No. Not yet. There'd be no recovery if she surrendered to the pain.

She pushed herself up and walked out to the living room. Her four-foot artificial Christmas tree lay on its side next to the window, ornaments scattered in a haphazard perimeter. Those that weren't crushed clung to the branches. Her gaze landed on the little wooden whale positioned halfway under her bookshelf. She crouched down. "That's it!"

Slade had followed her, and clashing emotions warred across his handsome features. He squatted beside her and shook his head. "It's a lot smaller than I imagined. And we can't touch it until after the investigators collect their evidence."

"How long will that take?"

"Depends."

An argument lingered on her lips, and she continued to stare at the item. "Zander had lost so much weight from his drug use, I barely recognized him. I told him God would help him if he only asked, but he laughed it off. That wasn't new. He'd mocked me about needing a crutch whenever I went to church."

Zander also promised to make her fall in love with him again. There was no chance of that happening, but Slade didn't need to know that part of the conversation. Her voice quivered. "If I'd been a better Christian, or wife, maybe he wouldn't be—" Her heart plummeted from familiar guilt again.

"Hey, don't do that to yourself." Slade tugged her into his arms.

This time, she succumbed to his embrace, allowing the warmth and protection he offered. She soaked in his acceptance and pushed away the years of rejection she'd harbored too long. "It's stupid to think I could have stopped his addiction, but the guilt is easier to deal with than admitting he loved drugs more than he loved me."

"I don't believe that. He was sick and blind. You're so worth loving," Slade assured her, his breath hot against her ear.

She had to establish distance before the moment lingered. Yet she didn't move.

His phone rang, providing the necessary separation. Slade released his hold on her and stood. He spoke quietly and turned his back to her, moving into the hallway.

Asia stretched her sleeve over her hand, creating a barrier, and seized the whale. She needed answers now, not later. She slid the item into her hoodie pocket. What Slade wasn't aware of, he wouldn't report. At least not yet.

Slade returned. "Beardly's on his way up."

Asia nodded, thankful he couldn't see her heart thudding inside her rib cage. "How did he know—"

"Good question." Slade moved toward the door. "Let me do the talking."

Asia trailed behind him, determined to smuggle the figurine out of the apartment undetected. Her pulse increased at the sight of Beardly closing the distance between them. She kept her hands in her hoodie pocket, wrapped around the whale.

"Trooper Jackson, Mrs. Stratton. I didn't expect to meet you here."

"We were just leaving."

Beardly blocked the path. "Imagine my surprise when I recognized the address on the request for an evidence tech. Good thing I was already in the neighborhood."

"Sergeant Oliver suggested we have Asia visit her apartment to see if the familiar surroundings would help her memory return."

Beardly narrowed his beady blue eyes. "Hmm—and did it?"

"Walking into the aftermath of a tornado deterred us," Slade responded.

"That's too bad. No twinge of memory at all?" Beardly addressed Asia.

"No, sir," she squeaked under his penetrating gaze.

He spoke to Slade. "Home invasion?"

"More like a desperate search for something, based on the way they destroyed her belongings."

"No kidding? What do you suppose they were looking for, Mrs. Stratton?"

She swallowed. "I have no clue."

"Well, it's a good thing you weren't at home when it happened. You could've been seriously injured." He pinned her with a glower. "You know, the DA has been quite interested in this high-profile case."

Asia maintained her position, afraid to draw attention to the whale that seemed to weigh a hundred pounds in her hoodie pocket.

"I've heard that. I'm sure you're eager for a solid lead

on the real killer." Slade's steely tone added to the palpable tension.

"We're closing in on a viable suspect. I'm anxious to make the arrest."

The cold air kept Asia from completely suffocating under the unspoken accusation.

"Well then, we'll let you get to work." Slade ushered Asia past Beardly.

He restricted her departure, stepping in her way. "Trooper, I may have further questions. Perhaps you should stick around."

The whale in her pocket grew heavier by the second. Asia turned to Slade. "I'm sorry, but my shoulder hurts. I should rest."

Beardly's feigned compassion was nauseating. "Of course. You're still recovering from a terrible series of events. Please go on ahead. I'll be in touch. I hope you feel better soon." He shifted enough for them to pass, but Asia felt his stare on her.

She didn't realize she'd been holding her breath until she exhaled on the last stair.

Trey met them in the parking lot. "What was that all about?"

"Beardly's intimidation games," Slade growled.

"I'm amazed at his response time. That's got to be a new record," Trey replied.

"Yeah, makes me wonder…"

Asia remained silent while the men conversed, impatient to get into the car and inspect the whale.

"We're headed back to the house."

"Roger that." Trey released Magnum. "We'll go *help* Investigator Beardly."

Once she and Slade had driven a block from her apartment complex, she spoke. "That man makes me nervous."

"Yeah." Slade gripped the steering wheel.

Asia retrieved the whale, catching a glimpse of Slade's double take in her peripheral. "What did you do?" he asked.

"Not sure yet." She turned the object over in her hand. "There's an opening." She inserted her fingernail and tugged, sucking in a breath.

"What's wrong?"

Asia withdrew the strange square item. "There's a key."

"I told you not to touch anything." The curiosity in his tone overrode the scolding in his words. "Do you realize what would've happened if Beardly knew you'd taken that?"

"Yep. I'm not waiting on everyone. I need answers now. And it seems I have one. Besides, I used my sleeve, so technically, I didn't violate your rules."

Slade shook his head and sighed. "What's that for?"

She passed it to him for inspection. She'd seen these before, but it wasn't a key for a regular lock. More like a—

"Locker key! Zander worked out at the YMCA all the time."

He grinned. "Well, I can't say I agree with your method, but good job. Guess that's our next step."

SEVEN

Before she talked herself out of it again, Asia asked, "I'm sure I'll regret this, but why aren't you more upset with me? I took the whale before the evidence people did their thing. Why the sudden change in your by-the-book ways?"

A shadow passed over Slade's face. What was he hiding?

"Does this have something to do with the call you got at my apartment?"

"No, that was Trey letting me know Beardly had arrived." Slade merged onto the highway leading out of town. "Trey's handling the report on your apartment, and the evidence folks will be busy documenting everything. So we'll maximize our time and deal with that key. However, since you mentioned it…"

Asia rolled her eyes. Here it came, Slade's tiresome attempt to talk her out of investigating her own case. Give the man an A for effort. "Don't waste your breath. I'm doing this with or without you."

Slade's lips flattened. "Before you get angry, let me explain my next statement. I'm all for discovering the locker contents ourselves, but it's in your best interest to have Beardly gather the evidence. We could have him meet us there to witness the discovery. Then if we encounter unwanted visitors, we'd have backup."

No way, Procedure Boy. Asia sat up straight, shoulders back. "I am not handing this key over to anyone until I see the contents for myself first."

"Asia, this isn't up to you—"

"Absolutely not. If you try to force me, I'll…I'll…" She'd what? Swallow the thing?

Slade lifted a hand in surrender. "Relax. Don't get yourself in a tizzy."

"Funny. Give us a little time to work through this before you go back to your straitlaced ways."

"For the record, I let you take the whale."

"You didn't *know* I'd taken it."

"Fine, but I also didn't make you return it to the scene."

"And I appreciate that." A twinge of guilt inched up her spine for putting Slade in a bad position. "Whatever the ramifications, I'll own them. You can deny any knowledge of the key in the whale."

Slade's tone was harsh. "I'm not into using others as my scapegoats."

Asia nearly doubled over from the verbal blow. His comment was a dig for the way she'd dumped all her anger on him. The familiar comfort of defensiveness returned.

"Understand, we're withholding evidence—"

"We are not. Stop with the rules. We have no clue what's inside the locker. It could have Zander's old dirty socks." Yet, based upon what Slade had said, Zander died hiding the contents.

"Asia." His voice held a warning.

She ignored him. Until she discovered what Zander intended by giving her the whale, she wasn't inviting anyone else into her messed-up world. But what if the mysterious locker held drugs or money? Would she look guiltier?

Slade was risking his career and life for her. What right did she have to argue with him? She was no expert in spy missions. If this qualified as a mission. "I'll let you lead, but no reinforcements until we see what's in the locker."

"Fair enough." He turned left, heading out of town.

Where was he going? "The YMCA is the other direction."

The corner of Slade's lip curved upward. "Prudent pre-planning is necessary."

"Seriously?"

"Quenten's men seem to be a step ahead of us. Let's trip them up a bit."

"What'd you have in mind?"

He grinned and accelerated onto the highway. "An incognito operation."

The next closest town was twenty minutes away with a population of three hundred and didn't host an excess of shopping possibilities. Working to keep the bossiness from her voice, she offered, "The mall is also in the other direction."

"Who needs a store? My aunt loved costume parties. She'll have what we need in her basement."

He'd thought through their next steps and produced a creative idea, but failed to factor in the time delay. She bit her lip to keep from voicing her annoyance.

"You've witnessed firsthand the determination those men have to find whatever that card holds. They won't give up."

"That's for sure. Do you think the card's in the locker?"

"Maybe. Let's put distance between us and your apartment. Let them think we've come up empty-handed rather than lead them straight to the source."

"That does make sense."

He grinned. "Will you look at us? The cooperative dream team."

"Whatever." She shook her head, feigning irritation.

"For the record, I value your opinions and ideas. Sometimes—not often—they might even be better than mine."

"I'm so glad you recognized that. Now I don't have to pretend complacency." She settled in the seat.

"I have sisters, remember?"

"You're well indoctrinated. Remind me to thank them." Not that she'd ever follow through with that commitment. Existing within the wild and entertaining Jackson clan, who laughed a lot and loved hard, had been great seventeen years ago. Acclimating to the perfect family now was inconceivable. Truth be told, she'd never belonged in their world. Or with Slade.

Asia bit her lip, wanting to ask the tough questions. When did the clock run out on her freedom? Would he arrest or just detain her? The answers wouldn't help though.

Other than the fact they were running for their lives, being in his company had become easier, as if no time had passed between them. But a lot of time *had* passed and left demolished dreams, broken hearts filled with loss and changing goals. The familiar whispers of doubt reminded her of the way Slade had betrayed his partner, and in doing so, he'd betrayed her. Asia closed her eyes, trying to focus on anything except the painful thoughts demanding attention.

No. She wouldn't go there. She must remain in the present, not lost in the past. No matter how many times she'd pushed Slade away, beaten him with her hateful words and accusations, he'd been there for her. Even to the point of responding to a bizarre message requesting he meet her at the decrepit mobile home.

Asia bolted upright in the seat. "Whoever sent you that text had knowledge of our history."

"I considered that too."

"A mutual friend or work contact? Or someone close to Zander?"

"Anybody come to mind?"

"No. Zander's issues left us without friends or community. I kept to myself. It was easier than having to explain his random binges and disappearances."

Slade nodded in understanding, and she caught a glimpse of the small scar on his right cheek. Before her head reasoned with her hand, she gently touched the healed wound.

"Proud of your tree-house-assault handiwork?" Slade asked with a grin.

She quirked a brow. "That's not fair. You're the one who talked me into climbing the stupid thing. It's not my fault you fell off."

He gave her a playful poke. "No way, Stratton. When I wasn't looking, you bumped—or pushed—me out of the tree."

She shook her head. "Hold on. We were eight years old, and as intelligent a child as I was, premeditating your fall from the tree wasn't on my agenda." She snickered. "But if that's what you need to tell yourself and everyone else, for the sake of your dignity, we can pretend."

The vehicle jolted into a pothole and she grasped his arm, the hard muscles unyielding beneath her touch. Solid and strong.

Slade turned to face her. "Sorry about that. Didn't see it coming until it was too late."

Couldn't have said it any better. Asia pushed back, then dropped her hands in her lap. Warmth radiated up her neck and her mind blanked.

For the first time since waking across from Nevil Quenten, the fear of prison wasn't what scared her most. It was the realization that she was softening toward Slade. Everything within her wanted to ignore his kindness and stay aloof, but the tug to embrace forgiveness pulled harder.

What had they been talking about? "Sorry, I'm still trying to get my heart rate down," she sputtered. True, but not for the reasons he'd be thinking.

"I'll pay better attention to the road," he promised. "Almost there."

She nodded while her mind continued to wander. Though it wasn't logical, she felt safe with Slade. Zander had left her to fend for herself, and the vulnerability had prevented her from sharing those fears with anyone. She couldn't afford visible weakness, even if it meant pretending strength. Being in Slade's care provided comfort, however fleeting it might be. The self-protection she kept in place guarding her heart shifted as she gave herself permission to trust him. She had no one else to turn to.

His friendship had been a lifeline throughout her tumultuous marriage—the only constant she depended on until Slade turned Zander in. Looking back, his timely demand that she end any communication with Slade explained a lot.

Her husband's facade of jealousy masked his true intentions. Zander stopped loving her a long time ago, so that hadn't been his motive. The truth dawned on her. He wanted to ensure she had no association with Slade.

Asia snorted, attracting Slade's attention. She coughed to cover the embarrassing noise.

Zander's misdeeds had merited reporting. Blaming Slade had been easier than admitting her husband chose everything except her. The rejection severed her confidence. His untimely death left her with a haunting, unanswerable question. Why hadn't she been enough?

"I sure hope this key is worth all the effort Zander took to hide it." And all he'd suffered to keep it hidden. Asia rolled the item in her hand. Did it hold the answers, or something more incriminating?

Asia lifted the blond wig from the bathroom counter and balanced it on one hand while using the other to finger-groom the wayward strands.

True to his word, Slade had found a large plastic tub filled with costumes in the basement of his aunt's home. They'd spent over an hour rummaging through the mixture of odds and ends to come up with a believable ensemble for each of them.

She tugged the hairpiece down over her ears, then tucked her own stray locks of dark hair inside. The wig's short wisps aged her twenty years and transformed her into a stranger. She slid a pair of black-rimmed eyeglasses on her nose and studied her appearance. Adorned in the navy business suit, she didn't recognize herself. Perfect.

A knock followed by Slade's baritone voice interrupted the inspection. "Ready?"

"Come on in."

The bathroom door swung open. Slade took a step forward then leaned against the frame, sporting a full graying beard, complete with matching eyebrows that sprouted above his round spectacle frames. His red-and-blue-striped sweater-vest complemented the khaki pants.

Asia tried—unsuccessfully—to stop the burst of giggles that escaped.

"I take it my disguise works?" Slade wriggled his eyebrows, making them dance above his glasses.

"Whew, give me a second." She wiped a tear from her eye. "It's perfect. You remind me of old man Jenkins. Although I think Trey will be our true litmus test." She smoothed down the jacket and fluffed her wig. "Let's do this."

Asia tucked her arm into his crooked elbow, and they made their way to the living room.

Trey glanced up from the newspaper he held, wearing a wide grin. "You two look great. Asia, you resemble Aunt Velma in that outfit. And, Slade…well…you're looking more like Dad."

Slade glanced down. "Yeah, I noticed that too."

Trey folded the paper. "Are you sure you don't want me to follow you?"

Magnum lay at his feet, his triangle-shaped head over enormous brown paws. He raised a furry eyebrow but didn't move.

"No, but keep your phone close. If there are any issues, I've got you on speed dial. We plan to be back within an hour."

"Alrighty." Trey lifted his paper again.

Asia aimed for the garage, but Slade grasped her arm. "We're riding in style." He pointed out the window to the seventies sedan—complete with chipping two-tone, blue-and-white paint and rusted everything else—parked across the street.

She paused. "Where did that come from?"

"I had it dropped off for us. I don't want to use Aunt Velma's car or Trey's. We need to keep Quenten's men guessing."

They walked out of the house and headed to the jalopy. Slade tugged open the passenger door, and it squeaked an unpleasant response.

Asia slid into the dusty interior, wrinkling her nose at the stale air. The cracked plastic seats revealed lines where yellowed cushion material peeked through.

Slade entered the driver's side, snapped his seat belt then started the engine. A loud screeching whine emitted from under the hood. "Needs a new serpentine belt," he explained.

"Are you sure this contraption is safe?"

"I hope so," he murmured.

They headed out of the small town and onto the highway. The lightheartedness they'd shared only moments before faded as they traveled across the rolling hills. The late-afternoon sunshine beat through the spider-webbed windshield.

Asia reached to turn on the heater, exuding dusty air from the vents. "I know you're wishing I'll stop asking, but I won't. What did Sergeant Oliver say when you talked with him last?"

Slade worked his jaw. "Not much."

"Humor me." Asia studied his taut expression. The quiet between them and the palpable stress had her anxiety escalating. "I can't take any more suspense. You have to tell me. Now."

"Let's handle this first area of business, get back to the house and then we can debrief everything to your heart's content."

"That's not ambiguous at all," she said sarcastically. "You're making it worse."

He frowned. "Later. I'm working through every scenario where this could go wrong."

Asia sighed. He was right, and he was avoiding the topic. Maybe knowing would do more damage than good. Was being overinformed bad? The thin, unrealistic rope anchoring her hope was better than nothing at all.

The drive went more quickly than she'd expected, and soon they parked in front of the colorful YMCA building, where a red LED sign boasted classes and events.

Slade turned off the engine and twisted to face her. "Okay, let me give you a final once-over."

Asia obeyed, and the full-on view of him had a grin tugging at her lips again.

"Stop it. Seriously, is anything out of place?" He scanned her too.

"Nope, you couldn't look more *not* like you if you tried," she responded truthfully.

"Excellent. Let's test it out, then." He shoved open his door.

Asia did the same, unwilling to wait for his gentlemanly assistance.

She took his arm, and they strolled along the mostly snow-free sidewalk to the building and entered through the glass doors. A teenage receptionist typed furiously on her phone. After several long minutes of being ignored, Asia cleared her throat, and the girl looked up, perturbed.

"Welcome to the YMCA," she mumbled in greeting before returning her attention to her cell.

"We'd like to see your building's fine amenities." Slade stepped forward.

"Are you a member?" The receptionist continued to text.

"No, we're hoping to check the place out first," Asia offered, fingering the locker key in her jacket pocket.

She glanced up and sighed at their intrusion on her valuable time. "I can show you around in a few minutes."

"That isn't necessary. You're obviously busy. Perhaps we could observe the facility for ourselves then see you if we have questions?" Slade asked.

"It's against policy." She sighed again, clearly bored with their discussion.

Asia opened her mouth to speak, but Slade placed a hand on her shoulder, then leaned over the counter. "I understand. We won't take long, especially if this place is as fabulous as we've heard."

Asia recognized his winning-the-girl-over tone.

Boisterous shrieks interrupted their conversation as a twentysomething woman with three rambunctious kids bounded through the doors. The children all bolted in opposite directions like minitornadoes, knocking over the fake plants in the lobby. They rushed to the windows that encircled the indoor pool and slapped their hands on the glass walls.

The woman's ponytail hung askew, and her frazzled expression testified it had been a long day. She ran toward one child, attempting to corral the youngster just as another squealed and sprinted in the opposite direction. "Joey, Suzy, Annie," she called, chasing after them.

"Hey, don't touch that," the receptionist said, pushing off her chair and moving out from behind the counter. She aimed for the oldest of the children, busy pressing buttons on the keypad that led to the indoor swimming pool. As she turned to deal with the offender, Slade ushered Asia away from the chaos.

"Act natural and stick with me," he whispered.

They hastened down the hallway to where a sign above two bright yellow doors read Men's Locker Room.

Slade stepped in front of the entrance. "Wait here."

Asia opened her mouth to argue but thought better of it and passed him the key.

"If you see anything suspicious, beat on the door and call, *Max, hurry up.*" He disappeared through the sunshiny door.

Asia leaned to the side and prayed no one came toward her, willing herself to act nonchalant. She bit her fingernail as a member of the rowdy mob bounded across the far end of the hallway.

Slade poked his head out the door. "Hey."

She jerked and pressed her hand to her throat. "You startled me."

He passed her a black letter-sized envelope.

"Let's get out of here before someone catches us."

"Chicken." Slade winked.

"Um, no, just respectful," she retorted, shoving the envelope into her pocket.

He chuckled, and they rushed down the hallway, nearly colliding with two approaching teenage boys. Asia dived behind Slade. *Right, they'll totally mistake me for a man.*

Slade whipped her around to face him and pulled her tight against him. He whispered, "Let them think we're kissing."

"Keep the flame alive, old-timer," the shorter one commented.

She glanced over Slade's arm, catching the taller of the pair elbowing his friend. The two pointed and laughed. Heat rose up her neck as the boys passed them and entered the locker room. At last the doors closed.

Slade still held her in an awkward embrace.

An unfamiliar flutter in her stomach had her pushing back. "Um, I think we're good," she said.

"Oh right. Sorry." Slade released his hold. "Great cover. Although an actual kiss would've been more believable." He peered around her into the hallway.

Embarrassed then riled, she considered retorting, but Slade's grip on her hand focused her attention. They hurried down the hallway then turned the corner.

He slowed and yanked her into an alcove.

Two men stood at the receptionist's desk, talking to the same girl still texting on her phone. The criminals who'd attacked them on the road.

Slade and Asia bolted back down the hallway.

"There's got to be another door!" he called.

They sped to a rear emergency exit. Slade triggered the fire alarm, then slammed his hands on the rectangular bar.

They burst through the door and ran down the sidewalk to the parking lot.

The car seemed a hundred miles away, and Asia had to dodge patches of ice and snow. At last, she slid into the passenger seat and the engine roared to life. Slade yanked the wheel, reversing in a J-turn before Asia finished latching her seat belt.

Her nervous gaze bounced from Slade to the front entrance. "Was that the wisest decision?"

The alarm continued to blare as the YMCA doors opened. The two men who'd been looking for them raced outside and scanned the area, caught sight of Slade's jalopy and lifted their guns.

The facility patrons stifled their attack, sprouting from everywhere in response to the alarm's demands. The men were swept up in the chaos of adults and children. Forced to tuck away their weapons, they ran to their vehicle.

Slade sped out of the parking lot, tires and serpentine belt screeching the entire way.

"They're coming!" Asia reported.

He shoved her down. "Duck!" A series of bullets pelted the car, and glass shattered around her.

Asia wrapped her arms over her head.

"Shoot back." He thrust his Glock at her.

She collected the weapon and slid up in her seat. Asia zeroed in on the vehicle barreling behind them.

It had been a long time since she'd fired a gun. *Hope it's like riding a bike.*

She rolled down the window, aimed and squeezed the trigger. The car swerved to the left then regained momentum. Asia released two more rounds.

Gravel and debris spewed up in front of the approaching vehicle's hood where the bullets made contact. A ting sounded off the metal bumper.

She fired again, this time hitting the windshield. The car veered onto the soft shoulder of the road and slid into the ditch.

Slade rounded the corner and sped away. He made several more turns onto county roads, ensuring he'd lost their pursuers, then headed to the highway.

Asia peered in the rearview mirror, confirming they weren't being followed. "I guess our disguises weren't as good as we thought."

Slade's foot pressed so hard against the pedal he worried it would go straight through what remained of the rusted-out floorboard. Why on earth had he agreed to the jalopy? Oh right, it was the only vehicle available in town on short notice.

They'd barely escaped the men and had been driving for twenty minutes through the country. He'd taken as many twists and turns as possible, ensuring they weren't followed.

When he'd put sufficient distance between them, he called Trey. "The creeps found us. Not sure how they tracked our location but I'm tossing the burner. Just wanted to keep you in the loop."

"I'll pick you up. Where are you?" Trey asked.

"Ten miles north on Highway 20 near Wayne."

"Okay, wait for me at the deserted gas station on Highway 20 and County Road 869."

"Affirmative." Slade disconnected and drove to the shoulder. He placed the phone under the tires and the satisfying crunch destroyed the device, ensuring it couldn't be traced.

"How did they find us?" Asia asked.

"The cell was a prepaid, so it shouldn't have been an issue, but I'm not taking any chances. We're ditching this bucket of rusted bolts and riding to the house with Trey."

"Good." Asia passed him back the gun.

"Nice shooting, by the way."

"I didn't hit anything or anyone."

"You made a favorable impression." He drove to a side road. No point in going straight to the gas station, since it would take Trey at least a half hour to reach them.

"Do you think it's safe to tear into this thing?" She held up the envelope.

"Safe? I'm not sure. Necessary? Absolutely." Slade pulled up behind a grove of trees and parked. He positioned them so he could see any oncoming cars and left the car running.

"Okay, here goes." She ripped apart the seal and peered inside. Disappointment and confusion intertwined in her expression.

"Well?" Slade resisted the urge to snatch the envelope from her hands.

"This is the card?" Asia held a blue SD memory card between her thumb and forefinger.

"Not what I expected either. Does the paper explain anything?"

Asia seemed lost in thought, tracing the sheet with her finger. Was she reading? Was there a picture? He cleared his throat to get her attention, but she sat transfixed by the white document. Several anxious minutes passed.

Finally, she swallowed, and her lip quivered.

An unexpected emotion clenched his heart. He wanted to pull her into his arms and comfort her. Instead, he gripped the steering wheel and watched for enemies, allowing her a few moments of silence to process whatever had captivated her.

When he'd counted to a hundred and checked the dashboard clock for the tenth time, he whispered, "Asia?"

She flinched as if he'd poked her. "Sorry, that caught me off guard."

"What did?"

"Seeing Zander's handwriting." Asia took a deep breath, flattened the paper and read aloud for Slade. "'Deliver this memory card to the man from Mrs. Camp's favorite Bible story. Only to him. If you fail, everything I did will be for nothing and your life will be in danger.'" She snorted. "He's a little late on that part."

Impatience pricked at Slade. He shifted into trooper mode, distancing himself from the events to gain the information he needed. "Okay, who's Mrs. Camp?"

Asia hesitated. "Zander's childhood Sunday school teacher."

Zander had gone to church? Since when? "I don't remember anyone by that name back home."

"No, this was long before he moved to our town. It's from when he lived in Spencer. Zander loved her. She was very kind and doted on him. She died of cancer when he was nine. Broke his heart. Zander said if there was a God, He'd have healed Mrs. Camp because she was the only person who'd ever loved him."

Slade sucked in a breath. "Oh, wow." Had he even known Zander?

"Yeah."

Back to interrogation mode. "Do you happen to remember her favorite story?"

"Give me a second." Asia closed her eyes, then sat up, eyes wide. "Yes! Jonah and the whale. That makes sense now. It's why he chose the whale figurine."

"We're making progress. Now, who's Jonah?"

She shrugged. "I don't know. There's a number printed at the bottom."

"Let's call." Slade reached for his phone and slapped the steering wheel. "Forgot I tossed it."

Asia studied the note again. "Why would he leave this for me?"

"Is there anything else in the envelope?"

She passed the document to him but held on to the card. He inspected it, wishing he'd remembered to handle it without contributing to the fingerprints Evidence would find. Too late now.

Uncomfortable at the sight of Zander's familiar scrawl—like it was his voice reaching from the grave—Slade returned the sheet to her, unable to continue reading. She might forgive him someday, but for Slade, there remained regret in everything Zander related.

Suspicion clawed at him, and questions blasted through his mind faster than he could process them. Had Zander played them? Was Jonah another drug runner? Asia's history with Zander revealed things he knew nothing about. Maybe conveying Zander's secret would help them put the pieces together. But how did all this relate to Quenten's murder?

He swallowed. No. If he said too much, too soon, his suspicions could do more damage than good.

"What are you trying not to say?" Asia placed a hand on his arm, whisking him back to the present.

Slade twisted so he faced her. Her dark eyes filled with questions. He shoved down the ambiguous answers he couldn't—no, wouldn't—give her. Yet. His stomach clenched. "It's been a crazy day. Let's find out what's on that card."

Asia pressed her lips tightly together, erecting an invisible wall of self-protection. He'd take her disappointment over putting her in further danger.

Slade glanced out the window. Not a car in sight. He shifted into Drive and turned onto the road. Images of Zander flashed before his eyes, visions of a twisted horror movie. "Honestly, I'm learning more about Zander's character than I care to admit. He was a strong man."

"I'm going over everything I remember about the last conversation we had. Zander seemed so sincere. I mean, he'd made promises before, but this time, it was like he was desperate. He'd never been that way before."

Slade swallowed hard, remembering his last visit with Zander and the promise he'd made under duress. He refused to meet her eyes.

"Did he suffer? You know what? Never mind. Forget I asked. I don't want to know."

Good thing, because Zander's crime scene was the last thing he wanted to discuss.

Asia shivered and tugged her winter coat tighter. "The night Zander gave me the whale he was nervous. His leg bounced the whole time, and he kept checking his watch."

Slade held his breath. Had Zander told her? "Did he say where he was going?"

"No. Just that things would be different, but there was something vulnerable in him."

He released the breath.

A truck stop on the side of the road caught his eye. He pulled in, parking around the rear of the building. "Wait here."

Slade rushed inside and purchased another burner phone. He kept Asia in his line of sight the entire time as he paid the cashier and ran back to the car.

He tossed the phone to her. "Dial for me, please."

"Zander said *I* needed to contact Jonah." Her eyes were wide.

"Trust me."

She did as he requested. Two rings and it went to voice mail with an automated response. "Jonah, I have a message from Zander. Call back at this number." He disconnected.

"Why not give him your name?"

"I'm guessing Jonah knows a lot more about us than we do about him. If that's true, he's been waiting for our call."

EIGHT

After considerable persuasion and a hint of begging, Asia convinced Slade to withhold the SD card details from Trey. Men's voices outside the bathroom motivated her to dress quickly after her shower. If the brothers spent too much time together without her present, Slade might succumb.

"Perfect timing," Slade said as she entered the living room.

"Really? For what?" She dropped onto the chair across from him and continued towel drying her hair.

Slade seemed to study her. Did she look that bad? What was his deal?

Conscious of her looks, she glanced down. The sweater and jeans—courtesy of Trey's shopping trip—were comfortable, not sloppy, despite the horrible olive green color. She didn't have makeup to wear. Perhaps a few minutes with a blow-dryer would've improved her run-down appearance?

Magnum moved to her side, and she stroked the dog's coarse fur. Though intimidating in appearance, he responded to her whispers of affection.

"I think Magnum's made a new friend," Slade said.

Trey laughed. "He's a ladies' man for sure. Don't get used to that, buddy."

"Stop it. He's great company," Asia defended him.

"Trey and I've been talking," Slade began.

He'd told his brother about the SD card. Irritation radiated throughout her body. They'd dismiss her from helping in the investigation. "I don't think so."

Slade jumped in. "Hear me out."

"Break time," Trey announced, standing. Magnum's ears perked, and he walked to his master.

Slade held up his hands in a position of surrender. "I think—"

"You're not leaving me out of this." Asia's gaze bounced between Slade and Trey.

"This is an active investigation," Slade reminded her.

Trey remained silent. Smart man.

Asia's jaw tightened. "Yeah? Well, it's *my* life."

That seemed to break through Slade's armor. He sighed and rubbed the back of his neck.

Trey had the audacity to laugh. "Easy, you two. Why don't we—" His cell phone interrupted, turning his expression solemn. "Sorry, I've got to take this."

Magnum followed him into the kitchen.

Slade stood, then shoved his hands into his pockets. "I understand you want to be a part of all that's happening, but your safety takes priority."

Before she replied, Trey returned. "I have to leave. Sergeant Oliver's orders."

"What's going on?" Slade asked.

"Manhunt for a single male, armed and considered dangerous. Shot up a department store. I'll be back as soon as I can. Oliver said I'm the only dog unit nearby. Short staffing strikes again." Trey shrugged on his winter coat.

A shooter on the run would take precedence over surveillance and protection detail of a murder suspect. That was a no-brainer.

"No worries," Slade replied.

"We'll be back ASAP." He and Magnum headed out, and Slade locked the door behind them. The roar of his dually pickup confirmed they were on their way.

Asia focused on Slade. "Did you tell Trey about the SD card?"

"No."

Embarrassment trailed her momentary relief. She had to stop overreacting. "Now that he's gone, can we look at the SD card?"

"You read my mind." Slade disappeared down the hallway and returned with his laptop from the other bedroom.

Asia moved to his side on the couch, but she underestimated the distance and brushed against his leg. "Sorry about that." She shifted over.

"I didn't mean to stare earlier." He booted up the computer.

So she hadn't imagined the weirdness. "Yeah, what was that about?"

"Seeing you with wet hair reminded me of our summers at the town pool."

Asia's stomach fluttered at the reminder of their teenage romance. Young love. The moment needed a reply. Her brain ignored the order, leaving her dumbfounded and searching for an intelligent response.

Thankfully, Slade spoke and changed the subject. "Do you have the card?"

Asia jumped up and rushed toward the bedroom, snatching the item from the pocket of her discarded clothes.

Slade inspected the available ports on his laptop and groaned. "I need a reader."

Disappointment collided with her anticipation. She glanced around and spotted Trey's laptop case next to the couch. "Would Trey have one?"

"Let's hope so." Slade reached over and snatched the bag. He withdrew a small memory card reader and connected it to his laptop. "Voilà." He inserted the SD card, and Asia situated herself beside him—careful this time to keep a respectable distance—watching as the screen displayed a single video file. He double-clicked the icon.

The scene, though dark, wasn't indistinguishable, and revealed three men standing outside a building. They shifted, providing her a glimpse. "I recognize Nevil Quenten." An involuntary shiver coursed through her. The guy resembled a banker or businessman, not a bloodthirsty crime lord. "Who're the others?"

Slade frowned, his brows dipped in concentration. "I'm not sure. The display's too dark. But that one—" he pointed to the tallest man "—is familiar." The other guy kept his back to the screen.

The tall man passed a briefcase to Quenten, then crossed his arms over his chest, remaining silhouetted. Quenten opened the briefcase, exposing stacks of money.

Asia gasped. "I've never seen so much cash."

The vein in Slade's neck pulsed and his jaw went taut. "I have, and it usually designates nefarious dealings."

Quenten stepped into the dim light. "Can we trust our friend to ensure the next shipment travels undetected across the state?"

The man with his back to the screen shifted. "My contact believes his time has expired. He's become unpredictable. Remove him. Call it collateral damage." He entered the building, but the dim light shadowed his face.

"Consider it done," Quenten replied, and the scene faded to black.

Slade turned to face her. "It would be wise to duplicate this."

The request took her aback. "You're asking my permission?"

He lifted one shoulder. "More for your cooperation. Zander left the evidence for you, trusting your decisions."

His confidence emboldened Asia. "Go ahead."

Slade nodded and copied the file onto his hard drive. He removed the SD card and handed it back to her, then put the reader back into Trey's laptop bag.

She palmed the item. "I wish we could lighten the footage somehow, so we can see the other men."

"I'm not that talented. On the other hand, Trey has mad computer skills. If you'll allow me to share it with him…" Slade closed the laptop and placed it on the coffee table.

"Yes, if Trey is willing to help us, I'd be very appreciative." Asia pushed up from the couch and paced between the kitchen and the living room. "Who is the contact the man spoke of? Do you think it's Jonah?"

"Anything is possible at this point."

"Who's the friend they want to eliminate? Do you think they're referring to Zander?"

Something flickered in Slade's eyes. He lifted a bottled water from the coffee table and removed the cap. Was he stalling? He took his time and sipped.

"Slade?"

"I can't say definitively."

"What kind of answer is that?"

He shrugged.

"What are you keeping from me? It's obvious you don't trust me."

"That's not it at all." He opened the laptop again, shifting his focus from her.

She dropped back onto the couch then lifted the small blue card. All the attempts on her life were for this? "Zander loved developing escape plans and scavenger hunts."

"Uh-huh," Slade mumbled, distracted, as he watched the video again.

"He'd go into a store, restaurant or shopping mall and mentally map out a plan should a situation arise. Creeped me out, until I realized it was a game for him."

Slade ignored her.

"Jackson, pay attention here."

He glanced up. "What?"

"I think Zander made a way of escape with the locker contents." The urge to unload Zander's secrets warred with her promise to tell no one. She inhaled for courage. "He'd gotten in deep with Nevil Quenten and it scared him. I overheard their conversation once and Zander kept repeating, *I'll get it done.* I'm not sure what he meant, and when I probed for more information, he told me to stay out of it." Asia drew invisible circles on the couch cushion. "Before our separation, he did everything to keep that part of his life from me—even confessed he led two lives. He signed up for every drug task force shift, then disappeared for days afterward. Zander played Quenten's watchdog and ensured the loads traveled through the posts without getting pulled over."

Slade worked his jaw. "And I thought my opinion of Zander couldn't possibly be any lower."

"His life was a series of one bad choice after another. He'd forgotten how to do the right thing." Asia leaned back, fidgeting with her sleeve. "I've got more questions now than I did before. Like who recorded the video?"

"I'm confident it was Zander."

"Maybe you're right that it's time to hand everything over to the patrol."

Slade shook his head, surprising her. "Not yet."

Asia did a double take. "Did we just experience role reversal? Haven't you been the one insisting we stay transparent with the investigation?" Why was she egging him on?

Slade's stiffened posture sent a ripple of concern through her. "Zander didn't hand this over to the patrol for a reason. We're missing a piece of this puzzle."

She considered the argument. "That still doesn't explain why you've had a sudden change of heart. What aren't you telling me?"

"We need more information."

What was his deal? "And…"

"And the less people involved for now, the better." The vague statement provided no enlightenment, but something in his tone said that was all she'd get.

"The video doesn't exonerate me from Quenten's murder."

"Not yet. But it helps, and once we identify the other men, we may have clues as to who else was in that trailer with you."

"And if you don't want to involve the patrol, how should we do that?"

"You won't like my idea."

"And that matters since when?"

"We need Trey's expertise and that means sharing all of the information we have up to this point."

"I can't disagree there." What difference did it make now? She needed all the help possible, even if it meant inviting one more person into her nightmare.

Slade paced the small living room. His mind's paradoxical rationalizations had him answering questions with more questions. Asia had excused herself and gone to the spare bedroom to lie down. The distance allowed him time to process the information.

What had Zander planned to do with the recording?

Why hadn't he turned it over when he asked Slade to arrest him? Or shared the video when they'd met with Oliver? Zander had had many opportunities to help himself and his case. He'd chosen to hide the evidence instead. Why?

Slade hadn't realized Zander provided the criminals passage through Nebraska. The news wasn't surprising, but it was frustrating. He lay back against the recliner and pinched the bridge of his nose to combat the acute throbbing that pulsated from his eyes to his neck, physical symptoms of his guilt for not divulging the rest of Zander's secrets to Asia.

"You're awful quiet," she said, startling him.

"Sorry, I've got a killer headache." He cringed at his choice of words.

"Is there aspirin in the medicine cabinet?"

"Don't worry about it."

"I'll check."

Great, Jackson, you're supposed to be the one taking care of her, and she's having to nurse you. He rubbed his temples, hoping to silence the rebuking thoughts.

If the other men in the video were troopers, Zander's suspicions about law enforcement were justified. Once Trey worked his computer brilliance, they'd have the clues needed to bring down those involved. At least Slade prayed that would be the case. And until they had proof, involving the patrol prematurely was unwise. Slade determined to withhold the evidence…for now.

The video didn't explain Quenten's murder or vindicate Asia; however, it provided other people of interest. Beardly would be forced to investigate all the evidence, not just the overwhelming heap pointing to Asia.

Something about the shadowed men triggered recognition, but nothing specific. No matter how hard he searched his mind, he couldn't place them. In all fairness, over four hundred troopers served within the patrol. It was impossible to know them all. Slade had a newfound appreciation for Asia's frustration regarding her own memory loss.

"I found ibuprofen that hasn't expired yet." She walked into the living room and passed two brown pills to him. "Do you need water?"

"Yes, please." He didn't need a drink to swallow the meds, but he'd use anything to avoid her questions right now.

She headed into the kitchen and returned seconds later with a bottled water. "Remind me to thank Trey for stocking the cabinets. He'll make a great husband someday."

"If he ever finds a woman willing to put up with him," Slade quipped.

Asia moved toward the window and peered through the white plastic blinds. "It's almost suppertime."

His burner phone rang, and Asia pivoted, a pensive expression etched on her pretty face. Slade glanced at the screen. "It's Oliver."

"I'll go see if I can whip up something for dinner," Asia said, excusing herself.

Slade waited until she'd exited the room, then answered. "Sarge."

"Sorry about taking Trey, but I need him to work that manhunt," Oliver began. "Magnum's one of the best, and I'm certain they'll catch the perp."

"I have no doubt."

"I'll send them back to you ASAP."

"I understand. So far, it's been quiet here."

"Good."

Awkward silence hung between them. Oliver's out-of-character apologetic approach sent a wave of worry rippling through Slade. Was he stalling?

Slade flipped absently through a magazine, wanting to

ask questions yet terrified to hear the answers. At the point of bursting, he said, "So…"

"Jackson, can you maintain visual on Mrs. Stratton and position yourself so you've got privacy?"

Slade stood and walked toward the kitchen, peering around the wall separating the living room and dining area. Asia rummaged through the pantry, her back to him.

"Yes." He slipped into the hallway, moving to the master bedroom and partially closing the door. "What's up?"

"I had hoped we'd avoid this, but I can't keep putting it off." Oliver wasn't one to beat around the bush.

"What are you trying to say?"

"District Attorney Kramer just left my office."

Slade held his breath, dreading the next words. No matter what Oliver said, it wouldn't be good news. "I still have forty-eight hours," he blurted.

"He wants Mrs. Stratton arrested for the murder of Nevil Quenten."

Frustration exploded, and the argument tumbled out before Slade stopped himself. "Well, he can also want Santa Claus to bring him a new Ferrari, but here in the real world, we don't arrest people without evidence."

"My ten-year-old has temper tantrums too, and I don't tolerate those. Do you need to recuse yourself?" Oliver's no-nonsense tone grated. Whose side was he on?

"Sorry." Slade paused and counted to twenty. "What's his hurry to prosecute the killer of a drug lord?" His retort escaped, rebelling against every warning in his head.

"Compose yourself. I warned you I'd pull you in a nanosecond if you crossed the line from professional to personal."

Slade inhaled his next comment, then exhaled something like an apology. "Yes, sir. Two days without sleep is wearing on me."

"I understand."

No, you really don't. Slade scrubbed his face. "I'll get some rest tonight and be fine."

"Jackson, this isn't a vendetta for Kramer. He's looking at the big picture. He's got no investment in Mrs. Stratton."

Slade restrained his smart response.

"You know his mantra," Oliver continued.

"'No one's above the law'—his infamous zero-tolerance policy," Slade quoted. "With all due respect, we're handling this by the book. She hasn't been given special treatment." *Except for withholding a key piece of evidence, postponing her official questioning and the fact I'd mortgage my house and sell everything I own to pay for her legal counsel. Worst-case scenario, we'd escape across the border before I let her go to prison.* The thought gave Slade pause. Would he take those drastic measures to keep her from incarceration?

"He wants a press conference tomorrow evening to name her publicly as a suspect."

Slade punched the pillow on the bed, visualizing Kramer's face. "He can't tell us how to do our jobs. Evidence outweighs his votes."

"Reelection is right around the corner. The opposing side is not pro law enforcement. Kramer's concerned his responsiveness to this case will make or break him."

"As if we should care about that."

Oliver coughed. "I don't disagree with you, but I also don't have the final say. Captain's hammering on me too."

Slade paced and dropped his voice to a whisper. "He's doing this as punishment for Zander's misdeeds. How long will the rest of us pay for one man's bad choices?"

Oliver sighed into the phone. "Jackson. Trust in the system."

Hadn't he told Asia that same thing in the beginning? His faith in the system was dwindling, and if Asia went to prison for a murder she didn't commit, the system would be a pathetic failure. "If she's even named as a person of interest, the press will thrill in baking her. They'll destroy her reputation regardless of whether she's cleared afterward."

"Probably."

"Sir. Perhaps it's time to let Kramer in on Zander's suspicions."

"I can't do that. Zander delivered no substantial evidence to prove his accusations. We'd all be eating crow's eggs."

A grin tugged at Slade's irritated lips at Oliver's confusion of the two clichés. He ignored it, focusing instead on his frustration. "You and Zander left me out of the plans. If you'd been straight with me, I could've protected him. I know this isn't a good time, but I need any information I can get that will help me with Asia's case. What happened before his murder?"

"Zander had the contacts he needed. You and I had to stay as far from that situation as possible."

"He's dead!" Slade's voice rose in volume, and he spun and faced the hallway, grateful it remained empty. He swiped his hand across his face.

"Jackson, if there was anything I thought would help Mrs. Stratton, I'd do it. Zander's claims were unsubstantiated. We're third party to his accusations, and defending a known conspirator with one of the biggest drug cartels in the country isn't something either of us can afford to fall on his sword over. Everything Zander offered was hearsay, and let's be honest, the man had an overwhelming propensity to lie."

Slade bit his cheek. Should he tell him about the video? There was no proof that Zander shot the footage, and other than the meeting, it proved nothing positive or negative for Asia. Unless they identified the other men. No. He needed evidence. Once they'd met with Jonah and Trey lightened the video, he'd risk that whole falling-on-his-sword thing.

"Listen, there's something else."

And the hits just keep on coming.

"Asia's clothing came back positive for gunshot residue."

"You're sure? Can Omaha run the test again? Could've been a false positive or leftovers from being near Quenten's body?" Slade fisted his hands so tight they cramped.

"I'm sorry to be the bearer of bad news, but the evidence proves she fired Zander's gun."

Slade's stomach twisted into a hundred different knots. This was getting more impossible by the second. "Do you have any good news for me?"

"I wish I did. I ordered the results to be delivered to me."

"Beardly will see them."

"Eventually. Paul Wittington owed me a favor. I can't withhold anything, but I can postpone sharing them for another twenty-four hours."

Wittington was the most decorated evidence technician in the state. His signature alone garnered respect. And sealed Asia's fate. "Did Omaha find anything that would help Asia?"

"Right now, no. If she remembers details about how she got to the trailer or the murder, it might behoove her. Even if it was a self-defense plea."

"But the scopolamine, the gunshot wound, the head laceration, the repeated attacks on her life—"

"Yes, her attorney will need to work those angles, but cold, hard evidence overrides her amnesia."

"She asked me for some names."

"I'll get a list of reputable attorneys over to you. You've been put through the wringer. Rest tonight. It's possible that tomorrow she'll have a burst of memories that'll shed new light."

"Or an arrest," Slade countered.

"Hang on." Oliver spoke in the background, the crackle of his radio bouncing over the line. "Manhunt is about over. Trey will return to you once he finishes his reports."

"Well, that's the first positive thing you've said all night."

"Don't give up hope, Jackson. Justice wins."

"Kramer's forcing his own idea of justice on us. Please allow me until tomorrow before I bring her in."

"Granted, but no later than noon. I'll be in touch." Oliver disconnected.

The last of his spent energy left his legs, and Slade yielded to the force of gravity, landing on the edge of the bed, still clutching the phone. The total weight of the hopeless situation bore down on his shoulders.

Kramer was a gutless wonder who loved the public spotlight more than serving the citizens. A primal protectiveness burned within him to prove Asia's innocence. For a fleeting second, he ran through the scenario of evading arrest and fleeing with her to Canada. Tonight.

He doubled over, hands flat on the floor. He wasn't a renegade. Or an outlaw.

But how was he supposed to hand her over?

Slade pushed up from the bed and walked toward the door, spotting the blue Bible on his aunt's dresser. He lifted the soft leather book and flipped through the well-worn pages.

He'd prayed earnestly for Zander and Asia. Did his prayers reach God? Yet where else did desperate men go?

Slade shuffled back to the bed and sat on the floral bedspread. *God, I have no answers and I'm not sure You're even listening. I took an oath to uphold the law. The law isn't working. What am I supposed to do now?*

Curiosity had slaughtered her heart. Asia's hands shook as she worked the manual opener over the can of pork and beans. Why hadn't she stayed in the kitchen and minded her own business?

After Slade's departure into the bedroom, an obnoxious need to snoop on his conversation had beckoned her to hide out in the bathroom and eavesdrop. She'd only heard bits and pieces from his side, but his condemning words about bringing her in had been enough. She'd made a silent retreat to the kitchen, pretending to care about a meal she didn't intend to eat.

And she had no one to blame but herself. On a positive note, being nosy had saved her from making a complete fool of herself. To think, she'd almost allowed her heart to care for Slade. How stupid would she look doing that now, right before he arrested her? He'd assume she was trying to manipulate him.

Asia shoved the can away and placed both hands on the edge of the counter to steady herself. Anger and fear swirled like tie-dyed colors blurring her vision. Worse, the familiar sting of betrayal pierced her heart. She'd counted on Slade. Once again, she'd been stupid enough to trust a man.

Asia grabbed the pork and beans, ramming the can opener into the lid and searing through the aluminum. She cranked the handle, taking out her fury while questions fueled each movement.

She had no right to be upset with Slade. He'd never pretended to be anyone other than his rule-follower self. Friendship meant nothing to him if someone broke the law. He'd sided with justice. Hadn't Zander's arrest been proof enough?

Yet…Slade had gone to the YMCA, withheld the SD card from Trey and stood loyally beside her. He'd had the opportunity to take her in a hundred different times already. The image of his handsome face and boyish grin confronted her. Asia paused, remembering their escape and the lightheartedness they'd shared.

"Hey, sorry about that. Oliver was giving me an update." Slade entered, infringing on her quiet debate. Was it her imagination, or did his voice quiver?

Feeling guilty, Procedure Boy? She forced a casual smile, one she'd learned to wear around Zander. She wouldn't let on that she knew anything. She grabbed a dishrag and wiped the already clean countertop.

"So what did you find to eat?" Slade opened the refrigerator and buried his head behind the door.

His nonchalant manner infuriated her. *Two can play this game.* "Hot dogs with pork and beans." She allowed the lightness to permeate her tone, though the mere thought of food turned her stomach. "Will Trey be here tonight?"

"Yes. Oliver said he'd come back as soon as he finished his reports."

Hopefully Jonah called before Trey returned. Regardless, she'd excuse herself to bed. Fake a headache. Then slip out the window. She'd call Jonah from a burner cell phone. Why wait on Slade?

They prepared the simple meal together, passing each other in a silent waltz around the kitchen, exchanging pointless conversation. Asia's resentment grew with every unspoken word. He'd promised to be straight with her. To help her. But he was pacifying her. He'd copied the video and would turn it in, along with arresting her.

In all the years enduring the pain of Zander's extramarital affairs and drug-induced binges, she'd never felt more alone than she did sitting across from Slade at the dining table now. Asia zoned out on his babbling chatter, unable to feign interest. Anger wouldn't help anyone. It might make him suspicious of her. Or provide motivation to rid himself of her earlier than planned. No, Asia would do what she'd done most of her adult life: pretend everything was okay while she fell to pieces inside.

Then she'd clear her name. By herself.

Slade continued rambling about something irrelevant. "So then I—"

"Why won't you tell me what Oliver said?" The words were out of her mouth before she could stop them.

His expression went blank. Using his fork, he absently shoveled the food around on his plate. She refused to look away, willing him to speak.

"We've got a new obstacle."

Asia leaned back and crossed her arms. "I'm listening."

Slade dropped his fork. "District Attorney Kramer has demanded your arrest and wants to hold a press conference."

She blinked, processing the information. Kramer would name her a killer in public. Her stomach bottomed out. "But there's no proof—"

"The lab tests confirmed gunshot residue on your clothing."

Understanding slammed into her with the weight of a three-hundred-pound linebacker. "So I shot Quenten?" She jumped up from the seat, ready to vomit. "No. No."

Slade moved to her side. "Listen, remember what I told you about scopolamine?"

Asia nodded. "It keeps a person compliant and leaves them with little or no memory of the event."

"Essentially, a person under the influence wouldn't have the ability to fight or refrain from doing whatever they were being instructed to do."

"So someone drugged and convinced me to kill him? And I did?" Asia gripped the table for support.

"It's possible."

She shoved away from him and paced in front of the counter. "I need a lawyer."

"Oliver promised to compile a list for you. But, Asia, I'm not giving up. Once we identify the men in the video, we'll have another clue. It could be a game changer."

She swallowed and lifted her chin. "So you told him about the card?" Even after he'd promised he wouldn't?

"No. I think it's in our best interest to meet with Jonah first."

The man continued to surprise her. "What if Jonah doesn't call?"

"He will."

"You sound awfully sure."

Slade shrugged.

"Then what?"

"We'll take the next steps."

Asia bit back her reply. *You already know your next steps: dump me off at the prison doors and go your merry way.*

"There's something I haven't been honest with you about."

Her head jerked up, and she focused on Slade, dread clinging to her shoulders. How much more could she endure?

"Oliver's concerned that I'm too attached to you and this case. He doubted my ability to separate our history from the circumstances."

Not where she'd expected him to go with this discussion, but okay. "And have you had trouble?"

"Yes." Slade returned to playing with his food, taking far too long to respond.

Asia fought the urge to prod him to continue. Wait. Was he handing her over to Beardly? Her stomach tightened.

"I realize this isn't the best time to tell you this—"

She held her breath. This was it. He'd pass her off like an insolent child so he wouldn't have to do the arrest. Determination squared her shoulders. Even more reason to leave tonight.

"Oliver's right. I have feelings for you."

Asia did a double take. *Say what?* She opened her mouth to speak but nothing came out.

Slade's cheeks reddened, giving him a youthful appearance. He hunched over, fidgeting and focusing on the table. "I can see that's not what you expected."

You have no idea. Asia swallowed the rock in her throat. "Okay…" Her mind swirled. He'd told Oliver he'd arrest her in the morning. So why tell her how much he cared now? Just another manipulation technique to wear down her defenses, no doubt. But the tiniest doubt lingered. Or did Slade have romantic feelings for her? Had she once again dubbed him the adversary and wound up mistaken? No, someone who cared about her would tell her the truth, not placate her until he arrested her.

He dropped the fork with a *clink* and took both of her hands into his. "I wanted you to know. I realize how unprofessional it is for me to tell you this, especially right now."

This time she was the one avoiding his eyes. He had some nerve.

"Hey, it's all right. I didn't expect you to jump up and declare you felt the same way."

Butterflies in her stomach burst into motion. Did she feel the same way?

Absolutely not. Slade had betrayed her. Planned to turn her in.

"I care for you."

She had no clue how to process these four words from him. Her brain chanted, *He isn't trustworthy.* But the memory of her hands nestled in his melted her reservations. It'd been so long since anyone had professed to care for her. So long since she'd been held. His eyes—gentle and sincere—searched hers and made her want to surrender.

"Hey, guys, sorry I took forever," Trey said, bursting through the front door. "I brought food though."

Asia jerked back.

Slade dropped her hands and jumped up, knocking over his uncapped water bottle.

"I'll get it." She bolted to the kitchen, grabbed a towel then worked to mop up the mess.

The men strode to the table, and Trey set down a large brown paper bag, from which wafted the delicious scent of hamburgers.

"Those smell great," Slade said, his tone a little too enthusiastic. "And you saved us from doing something crazy like eating processed food." He glanced at Asia and winked.

"You'd have to be insane to eat hot dogs. Gross," Trey concluded. "Magnum doesn't even like them."

"Right." Asia snorted. No. Crazy was her forgetting that an accused murderer and her arresting state trooper would never make a good match.

NINE

The rest of the evening passed uneventfully, though the obvious emotional distance hung thick between Slade and Asia. He and Trey tried engaging her in conversation, eliciting only single-word replies from her. She hadn't touched her food before excusing herself with claims of a headache.

Slade never should've told her about his feelings. *Timing is everything*, Pops would say, and Slade's timing was notoriously bad. At least he'd thought to obtain her consent in showing Trey the video.

Once the men had moved to the living room, Slade prepared to dive into the footage.

"Did I see what I think I saw earlier?" Trey reclined in the La-Z-Boy and flipped on the television, then turned down the volume.

"Don't know what you're talking about." Slade snatched his laptop and cued the file. "Let's deal with this video."

"Whatever, bro." Trey's eyebrows knit together, and he leaned closer to the screen.

"You see the familiarity too?"

"Yeah, but man, I just can't pinpoint who it is."

"Would you do your computer-whiz thing and lighten the footage?"

"I'll do my best. Is Oliver aware of this?" Resignation clung to Trey's words.

Slade sat up straighter. "Not yet." He provided Trey a rundown of Oliver's update and the order to arrest Asia in the morning. "We're running out of time, so if at all possible, it has to be done tonight."

"On it." Trey lifted his laptop and started clicking away at the keyboard.

Slade's phone rang, startling him. "Turn down the TV—it's Jonah."

Trey sat beside him, and Slade positioned the cell between them then hit Speaker. "Hello, Jonah."

"Identify yourself," the male's voice demanded.

"Slade Jackson."

"Ah, the infamous Slade."

"I beg your pardon?" Irritation eked up his neck.

"Zander forewarned you'd help Asia," Jonah replied. "Is she with you?"

"Yes."

"Where are you?"

Who was this guy? Another of Zander's loser drug connections? "Look, Zander might've given you the scoop on me, but he certainly didn't give me the same courtesy. I'm not divulging anything over the phone to a perfect stranger. Who are you?"

The man chuckled. "Zander said you'd react that way. Good. I like a suspicious person. Means you're as wary of me as I am of you. For now, you'll have to be satisfied with my first name. Meet me tomorrow at 0800. Only you and Asia and bring the SD card."

"Sorry, pal, but I'm not willing to go trotting off to meet some interloper. I want more information before I even consider bringing Asia. Let's start with the card."

"I'll play straight with you if you do the same, but no

info over the phone. And it's my card. You cannot bring anyone else into this. Too many lives are at stake."

"Yeah? Well, too many lives are at stake on this end too."

Jonah sighed. "I won't do this little tango all night. Tell you what. I'll up the ante. I have something that'll prove you need to meet me."

"And what's that?"

"Confirmation of Zander's suspicions…and details about his murder."

Slade sucked in a breath. "How do you—"

"Tomorrow, 0800. I'll text the location in the morning." Jonah hung up, leaving no room for argument.

Trey jumped to his feet. "He said 0800. He speaks in military time. Cop? Armed forces?"

"It's conceivable. Guess we'll find out tomorrow."

"Dude, this is insane. You can't just dart to some covert meeting with this guy! Someone needs to know."

Slade stood and slapped his brother's back. "*Someone* does know."

Trey shook his head. "No way. I don't feel good about this. Either you tell Oliver, or I will."

"Believe me, if I had any other solution, I'd take it. Jonah's running the show, and there are some very not-nice people hunting for this video."

"You're aware of the potential fallout from all of this, right? Like our jobs. If not our lives."

"Oh yeah, I've counted the cost. I totally understand if you choose not to get involved. We can pretend this discussion never happened." Slade studied his brother's expression. Had he put too much on Trey?

"I don't know—"

"I'm sorry. That wasn't fair. I shouldn't have dragged you into this." Slade stooped to pet Magnum. "Promise me one thing?"

"You're already overdrawn on your brotherly favors at the moment."

Slade grinned. "Charge me interest."

Trey rolled his eyes and dropped onto the couch.

"Whatever happens to me, please take care of Asia. Oliver's providing a list of reputable attorneys. Use up my bank accounts, sell my house, do what you need to, but make sure she has everything she needs. And if there's no evidence to exonerate her...get her to Canada."

"Have you lost your mind?" Trey hissed, bolting upright. "You cannot sacrifice your life and career for her. I care about Asia too, but this is crazy."

Slade scrubbed a hand over his face.

Awareness registered in Trey's expression, and he shook his head. "You still have feelings for her."

Unable to look at his brother, Slade concentrated on the beige carpet.

"No. You cannot cross the line from professional to personal. If Oliver suspects you've gone one hundred percent partial, he'll pass Asia over to Beardly."

Slade didn't answer. His confession to Asia had been interrupted, but she hadn't resisted. Had he taken advantage of her weakened state? "Doesn't matter."

"Oh, it matters."

"All I care about is Asia's safety. Please promise me."

Trey groaned and threw up his hands in a "whatever" gesture. "Family comes first. I've got your six."

"I need to talk to Asia." Slade crossed the room and stepped into the hallway. No light shone from beneath her closed bedroom door. She must be asleep.

Should he wake her or wait? The woman needed rest. They'd run nonstop since her release. Still...she'd demanded to be filled in on every detail.

Zander's case had gone cold too early in the investigation, and unlike Asia, he wasn't an innocent party. Yet he deserved justice too. Would Jonah reveal the identity of the other men in the video? And why had he called it *his SD card*? Regardless, Slade had a fail-safe copy.

He pressed his fingers against Asia's bedroom door as the internal debate continued, then concluded he'd wake her early tomorrow and fill her in on the details. She needed rest. They all did. Tomorrow he'd face the biggest decision of his life.

Trey's words resonated with him. Was he stupid to sacrifice everything for a woman who'd openly declared her dislike for him?

The endless hamster wheel of mind racing and eventful days left Asia exhausted. A twinge of guilt for contemplating escape battled with her longing to sleep. Time wasn't on her side—not that it had been since the onset of this never-ending nightmare.

She tugged the pillow tighter under her chin and rolled over, staring at the ceiling. "God, I give up, okay? I'm waving my little white flag of defeat."

If Slade heard her, he'd think she'd lost her mind. Or forty-eight hours of it that would cost her her life if she didn't remember, and fast.

She lifted the small blue SD card, turning it over between her fingers. The craziness of the day's adventures played like a comedy, from their ridiculous disguises to outrunning the shooters, finding the video and now waiting for the mysterious Jonah to return Slade's call.

And around again she went on the hamster wheel as questions ravaged her mind. Why hadn't Zander gone to the police with the evidence? Why sacrifice his life for something if it wasn't enough to save him?

She held up the card. What did this video prove? Should

she leave it for Slade? No, he'd made a copy on his laptop, and Trey would do whatever he did to enhance the images. She'd left them everything they needed. Surely her cooperation would be a mark in her favor, and perhaps they'd find something to clear her name.

Trey and Slade's soft baritone discussion was too quiet to decipher, not that she'd tried. One devastating eavesdropping session today was plenty. Besides, what difference did it make? Slade planned to arrest her in the morning. She had no choice.

Asia glanced at the bedside clock. Midnight. When would those two call it a night?

Finally, their voices faded, and several seconds later the neighboring bedroom door shut. Was Trey still in the living room? He'd stay and keep watch. At least she hoped so. If Magnum barked, though, that would be her undoing.

Patience was essential. She'd get one shot at escaping, so blowing that on a hasty exit was foolish. Her eyes grew heavy, inviting sleep, so she pushed up off the bed and crept to the window. Her hand stilled on the drapes. With a long inhalation, she peeled back a corner and determined her getaway route. The large rectangular single-paned glass would be easy to climb out of.

She frowned, realizing her winter coat hung in the living room. Why hadn't she thought to grab it earlier? Layering the hoodie over her sweater would have to suffice. Asia slipped the SD card into the whale's hidden compartment, then dropped it into her hoodie pocket for safekeeping.

Asia hesitated. There'd be no turning back once she left the safety of this house. Was she making a mistake? Her hopes hung on this mysterious Jonah and the expectation he'd provide life-changing information. Slade promised to tell her as soon as the man called, but that hadn't happened yet. Disappointment was a familiar friend. She wasn't waiting around anymore. She'd try contacting Jonah again when she was on her own.

She twisted, glancing at the door.

What if Jonah provided no help? Slade's words flitted through her mind. *Kramer's forcing his own idea of justice on us. Please allow me until tomorrow before I bring her in.*

No question—he'd arrest her because his job came before anything else. Ever the rule follower, Slade wouldn't go against Sergeant Oliver's orders. His sudden change in withholding the card from Oliver meant he wanted credit for the find. Once Slade arrested her, he'd return to investigating the case while she did time for a murder she didn't commit. Especially without the money for an attorney and no family or friends. She was alone.

Asia leaned her head against the cold glass, whispering her plea. "Lord, what right do I have to ask for Your help? But where else can I go? Please rescue me."

She released the drapes, and they fluttered closed. Time to make her escape. Asia tugged on her shoes and glanced at the clock again. Five minutes to one.

One last peek at the door. What was the best way to leave the house without anyone hearing or seeing her?

She returned to the window, and her finger bounced in nervous anticipation. Finally, she unlocked the latch. After several tries, she managed to tug it upward, tossing caution out with her common sense.

The shoved-out screen landed with a soft thump in the yard.

Asia listened for any sounds. Nothing.

Reason battled with fear. *Think. Where do I go from here? God, what do I do?*

The visual of Slade's heartfelt confession came to her, immediately squelched by the reminder that he and Zander had been best friends too. *Look what happened there.*

Slade saying he cared for her was nothing more than a selfish way of softening the blow when he arrested her in the morning. Just another infamous *Sorry, I've got to do this* excuse. She had to leave before he destroyed their relationship forever. She'd never forgive him for turning her in. This way, she'd chosen to be labeled a fugitive over a prisoner.

She'd return with evidence to clear her name. Nobody proved capable of protecting her from these psychopaths, especially in jail. She wasn't safe anywhere. Any illusion of security had been quashed at the hospital.

She thought of the little cabin tucked in Long Pine's forest where she'd grieved in seclusion after Zander's murder, away from the judgmental citizens of small-town Newman Valley. She had stayed, at least until she had run out of money and supplies, prompting her return to real life and her job, which the salon thankfully had held.

It was doubtful they'd hold her position again if she were incarcerated. The retreat to Long Pine became more appealing. She couldn't—no, she *wouldn't*—wait for the proverbial other shoe to drop.

Resolve fueled Asia's climb out of the window. She contemplated tugging the glass closed, then retracted her hand. What difference would that make? As if Slade wouldn't realize how she'd escaped?

Trey's vehicle sat in the driveway, but borrowing the dually wasn't possible. Walking would take longer, but she'd hitch a ride once she reached the highway. Asia surveyed her options, choosing to move toward the backyard and into the connecting alley rather than walk down the street in case someone saw her. No fence surrounded the property, and small spaces of dead grass peeked up where snow had melted in sections of the yard.

Asia used the dry patches to hopscotch her way to the

alley, pausing under the cover of the shadows beside a gardening shed. The similarity to her and Slade's escape the night at the mobile home wasn't lost on her, but there was no danger tonight. Not a sound came from the house, and the older neighborhood slept while adrenaline ravaged her veins in anticipation. A light flutter of snow flitted around her, feathering her eyelashes.

With a deep breath, Asia ignored the inner voice warning this wasn't a good idea, and spun on her heel.

She collided with a force that jerked her backward. Something clamped hard over her mouth.

Asia twisted, screaming under the gloved hand.

A pinch to her neck dropped her legs out from under her. Every nerve ending went numb. Weightless, her body ignored gravity as strong arms hefted her into the air and carried her away.

Slade snagged his gun, bolted upright and threw his legs over the bed. He peered out the window, certain he'd heard something, but spotted nothing. He opted for a glass of water and strode into the darkened living room.

Magnum's triangle ears were perked, and he emitted a low growl as he stood beside Trey at the front door.

"What's going on?" Slade asked as Trey tugged open the door.

Magnum bolted outside with the two men trailing behind him. The dog rounded the house and hurried to the backyard.

They caught up with Magnum in the alley. The dog paced back and forth in the same area, nose to the ground. Trey ruffled the dog's fur. "Something's got him worked up."

"Probably another cat." Slade yawned.

"Maybe..." Trey said with a twinge of doubt in his tone.

Slade surveyed the slumbering neighborhood. No unusual activity, lights or sounds. Just the ordinary quiet of Meadow Hills. They were safe. No one knew about this house except him and Trey. He hadn't even shared the location with Sergeant Oliver.

Yet Magnum's response left Slade unconvinced, at least partially. The trio returned to the living room and turned the lock. Uneasiness still burdened Slade. "Find anything useful?"

Trey sat up, pulling the computer onto his lap. "Not yet, but I'm getting closer."

"I need to talk to Asia." Slade sat in the recliner. The weight of the day pressed down on him, draining every remnant of energy from his exhausted body.

"Thought you didn't want to wake her?"

"I don't, but I can't sleep. She deserves to know. It's her life."

"I agree. She might be awake and staring at the ceiling," Trey said, fingers gliding across the keyboard. "First thing in the morning, you need to notify Sergeant Oliver too. Jonah's call is significant."

"You're not going to let that go, are you?"

"Nope."

Slade considered Trey's suggestion while walking to Asia's bedroom. In the hallway, he scrubbed his hand over his face, took a fortifying breath and rapped lightly on the door three times.

Magnum barked and rushed to his side. Wound this tight, Slade would never get to sleep. If his knock hadn't awakened her, the Belgian Malinois's throaty greeting would do the trick. "Asia? Wake up. I've got news."

No response.

Three more knocks.

One final thump and no reply had Slade opening the door. "Hey, sorry to intrude on you, but—"

An icy breeze and the waving curtains signaled him. He rushed to the open window and stuck his head outside. *No. No. No.*

He stormed to the hallway, heart thundering in his chest, and nearly bumped into Trey. "She's gone."

"What?" Trey pushed past him and entered the bedroom, Magnum at his side. "How's that possible?"

Slade spun on his heel, snatched his gun and flashlight off the nightstand and bolted through the front door, circling the house. There weren't footprints in the hardened snow, but the patchy areas provided viable places where she could've stepped.

Yet no sign of Asia. A chill ran up his spine that had little to do with the eerie calm of evening and the frosty breeze.

What had she been thinking? He jogged the perimeter, then out to the street.

Trey and Magnum worked the opposite side, making their way to him.

"She left voluntarily. The window was unlocked from the inside." Slade's anger spread throughout his body. "Why would she do something so stupid?"

"She's on foot and won't get far."

"Let's drive the neighborhood. I'll update Oliver." He lifted his cell phone.

Trey put a hand on his shoulder. "Wait. What if she got scared and took off? If we alert Oliver and he posts an APB on her, she'll be marked a fugitive."

His brother was right.

"No need to call the boss yet. We'll find her and talk some sense into her," Trey assured him.

Slade nodded and dropped the cell into his pocket.

"Magnum's got something." The dog tugged Trey back into the alley, nose scouring the ground.

Slade caught up to them and spotted the figurine Magnum alerted on. Slade stooped, dread flooding him, and picked up the wooden whale. Turning it over, he opened the small compartment and withdrew the SD card, then passed them to Trey.

"Maybe she was running, and it fell out of her pocket?" Trey frowned.

"It's possible, but my gut says she didn't leave voluntarily."

The ground shifted beneath her, combined with a hum, reminding her of Slade's hot rod Big Sally. The fogginess beckoned Asia, but she forced her eyes open and squinted against the glow of red next to her.

Brake lights. She'd been stuffed into the trunk of a car.

Her pulse increased, and she gagged on the sour fabric lodged in her mouth. *Breathe. Breathe.* She willed herself to calm down, focusing on the last events before her abduction. The getaway and pausing in the alley before the man grabbed her. Then a complete void. She'd never seen her kidnapper. Never had a chance to respond before he'd stabbed her with a needle, drugging her.

The weight of her body pressed her injured shoulder into the scratchy, sparse carpeting. Restraints on her wrists and ankles rubbed the tender wounds from the night before.

She focused on escape possibilities, keeping her mind busy to reduce her fear. Every car made after 2001 was required to have a trunk release. She knew that because she'd used it as a topic for a paper in college. All she had to do was pull the lever and escape.

Asia studied her surroundings. The car was old, and

with the dim light, she struggled to find the latch. And her hands were bound behind her back.

The vehicle slowed and Asia rolled forward. The driver accelerated and turned, sending her crashing into the hard plastic wall.

She blinked against the stinging in her nose.

The vehicle stopped.

Terror squeezed her chest, stealing her breath. Her pulse beat heavy in her ears. She wriggled, but there wasn't enough room to kick her feet free.

A door slammed. He was coming for her. Whoever *he* was.

Steps drew closer. Asia tried to swallow the fear, succeeding only in gagging again.

Who had her? What was going to happen? Why had she been so stupid? Slade would never find her.

This was it, her inevitable demise. She would die tonight.

I'm sorry, Lord, for everything. She'd walked away from God. Not completely, but enough that she'd hardened her heart, unwilling to trust Him again. Blaming Him for her choices and every bad thing in her life. Each disappointment added a brick to her wall, holding God at a distance. She'd convinced herself He wasn't trustworthy, relying only on herself. And where had that gotten her? Here. Residing in wounded isolation because she feared enduring hurt again. *I can't be alone anymore. Lord, I don't deserve Your forgiveness, but I'm asking.* A tear trickled down her cheek. *Help me face my death with courage.*

The footsteps stopped outside the trunk. An endless series of seconds ticked by.

Finally, the lid opened with a painful screech, illuminating a yellow light above her.

Asia blinked, absorbing the sight of the gorilla-masked man. He hovered, gun aimed at her.

"Ah, you're awake. He'll be glad to see that."

He? Asia tried to swallow, choking again on the gag.

"This was avoidable. All you had to do was give me the card at the hospital. I would've protected you from him. Now you'll face his wrath and likely die. Unless you co-operate. Then you might survive."

She blinked, focused on his eyes. Dark brown, shadowed by the mask.

"I'm going to lift you. If you don't fight me, I'll set you down nice and gentle. Make me mad and I'll drop you on your empty head. Got it?"

Asia nodded, her ear rubbing against the carpet.

True to his word, he reached in and grabbed her arm, hoisting her out of the vehicle.

She winced at the harsh treatment but remained compliant.

He set her gently upright on the snow-covered dirt road. The moon hung low in the sky, providing ample light, but the area was unfamiliar. Fear compressed the air from her chest like a boa constrictor was wrapped around it. She had no hope of rescue.

Asia squeezed her eyes shut. *Lord, I'm trying to be brave but I'm terrified. Why didn't I tell Slade I was leaving?*

"You're wise to follow instructions," he commended.

As if she had any choice. Worry swarmed her, and not unwarranted. She'd made a huge mistake. It would appear making the wrong decision had become her natural talent.

Asia fought her anxiety by working to memorize every detail of her location. If she managed to escape, she'd have to find her way back to civilization. *Focus.*

Anxiety morphed into confusion, increasing to full-blown fear as he turned her toward an aged two-story farmhouse. Only the howling wind blew through the trees. No lights of neighboring homes glowed in the distance. There was no one to run to for help.

Asia shivered. Why did her captor remain disguised? Who was the other man he referred to? He'd keep her alive until he got what he wanted. You don't negotiate with a dead person. She'd barter with him, convince him to take her back and promise to surrender the card. He didn't know the whale was in her pocket.

Focus before your minuscule courage completely flees. She studied the home. Light glowed from the kitchen window, beckoning her forward.

"Walk or I'll drag you by your hair." He pressed the gun into the small of her back.

Was the man inept? How was she supposed to move with her ankle restraints? He must've sensed her hesitation because he ripped off the tape, taking the rag with it.

Asia coughed, inhaling the frigid air. "Why are you doing this?"

"Don't play stupid. I'll remove the tape on your ankles. Try to run away and I'll shoot you."

"Okay," she choked out.

He seemed to consider her before placing the gun in his waistband. He removed a switchblade from his pocket and flicked it open, pausing, she guessed, to increase the terrifying effect. Finally, he knelt and sliced through the tape, freeing her to walk. He withdrew the weapon and poked her in the back. "Let's go."

She shuffled forward, studying the aged property in serious need of TLC. Her father called homes like this shotgun houses. Shoot through one end, and it went out through the other. She climbed the decrepit porch steps, wood creaking beneath her feet.

Her captor tugged open the windowed door, releasing

a wave of musty air. The hazy glow from the back of the living area welcomed them.

"Move." He shoved her from behind.

She stumbled into the kitchen, catching a glimpse of a butcher block with knives on the counter to the right. If only she could manage to free her hands, or at least get him to move them in front of her, she'd grab one.

"Sit down." Her captor pulled out a chair at the table.

Asia dropped onto the seat and glared at him. Her head continued to throb, along with her shoulder in pulsating beats. "What did you inject me with?"

"Something to keep you compliant."

"Scopolamine?" A fresh surge of fear smothered her with terrifying scenarios.

"Aren't you the little pharmacist? No, that's not my style."

"Have you been sent to kill me?"

He snorted and leaned against the wall. "Killing you would defeat the purpose of getting the card, now wouldn't it? Are you figuring out Zander had a lot of enemies? I'm not the only one who's coming for you. It would be best to work with me."

"If I tell you, will you let me go?"

He shrugged, and the action looked almost comical with his gorilla-masked face. "If the boss comes down here, you're dead for sure. With me, you've got a chance of surviving."

"Why?" Stupid question, but whatever kept him talking.

"Because you can't identify me."

The man was a liar. She was dead. Alarm gripped her heart.

"I've researched you, Mrs. Stratton. Widowed. No family. Best I can find, no real friends either. Would anyone notice if you were gone?"

Hurt tightened Asia's stomach at the hateful yet accurate assumption.

"So why not tell me? Who would it affect? No one cares about you. Make this easy on yourself."

"Slade does," Asia uttered.

"Ah yes, Mr. Walking Policy-and-Procedure Manual. Kudos to his creativity though. We thought you'd be thrown into prison by now."

Asia lifted her chin. "He'll find me."

"Really? And how will he do that? Is he aware you slipped out of your bedroom and tried to run away? You did make that too easy for me, by the way. Thanks." The trilling of a phone broke their standoff. The man jerked, apparently startled. "Not a sound or I'll silence you for good."

He wouldn't, at least not until she told him where to find the card. He'd have to remove the mask to answer. When he did, she'd tackle him. *And how will you pull that off with your bound hands?*

Her captor crossed the room and moved behind her, placing the gun to her head, conveniently against the stitches. "Move an inch and I'll shoot you without question."

She winced but remained motionless.

He paused, then said, "Yeah."

Asia strained to hear the caller's voice. The gorilla-masked man pressed the barrel harder against her healing wound. What did it matter? Even if she gave him the card, this goon had no inkling Slade had a copy.

She dropped her gaze to her hoodie. She didn't feel the weight, but the figurine was little. Was the whale still in there? Shifting slightly, she crossed her legs, bumping the hoodie pocket. Empty. She'd lost it! Hope exploded. Slade would find it and realize she'd been kidnapped. Until he saw the opened window. Then what? *Please, God, lead him to me and give me wisdom.*

"Yep. Perfect," the man said, still engaged in the phone conversation.

If she remained here, she was dead for sure. Slade wouldn't discover this remote farm. She had to get back to civilization, get someone's attention and escape.

Mask in place, the man moved around her, hovering. "So where is it?"

Maybe there was a way to bluff her way out of this mess. "Seems you and I were both placed in the middle of a tug-of-war over this card."

He stepped to the side, crossing his arms.

What she'd give to see his face. Was she getting through? Asia continued, "I'd be willing to bargain with you."

"Why would I do that?"

"Why not? I want to live. I never chose the responsibility of keeping that stupid card. Didn't even know it existed until I was framed for Quenten's murder. I want nothing more than to be rid of that albatross. But I need something in return."

"Too bad." He shook his head.

She pressed on. "Just think, if I gave you the card, and you agreed to let me go, you'd make your own demands. I haven't seen your face, have no way of identifying you."

"I don't know…"

Asia shrugged, confidence building. "Or kill me and you get nothing."

"How do I know you wouldn't tell the police?"

She snorted. "You mean the police who believe I killed Quenten? They're not going to help me, so why would I do that? Besides, if you have the card, I don't have anything of value for your boss, right?"

He tilted his head, and Asia had to keep from grinning at the silliness of his posture with the gorilla mask. He didn't ask about the video. Did he know what the card contained?

Would his boss reveal those details? Or was this hired kidnapper nothing more than brawn?

"I'll take you to where the card is, you can drop me off on the side of the road and we both get what we want."

He lifted his phone.

No. He'd call his boss and she'd never escape. "Demand enough money to leave the country. Go somewhere tropical."

He jerked up his head. "Okay, Mrs. Stratton, I'll take you up on your offer. But if you're lying or trying to trick me, not only will you die, but so will Slade and his brother Trey."

TEN

The gorilla-masked man shoved Asia into the back seat of the older-model sedan. Arms still bound behind her, she landed on her side and had to wriggle to an upright position. Irritated, she glared at him and demanded, "What about my seat belt?" When he leaned in, she'd headbutt him.

"Shut up or I'll gag you again. Try anything funny and I'll toss you into the trunk." He slammed the door then climbed into the driver's seat. "Where am I going?"

Good question. She couldn't return to the house where Slade and Trey were, so where should she have him drive? She needed to buy time and get to civilization. And at the moment, she had no idea where they were. How long had they driven when she'd been unconscious? "Newman Valley," Asia blurted.

Was he the ruthless destroyer of her home? Or one of the men who'd shot at them from the YMCA?

"*Where* in Newman Valley?" Annoyance oozed through his mask, and he glared at her in the rearview mirror.

She contemplated, then squared her shoulders. "My apartment."

"Nope. Already checked there."

Indignation boiled her blood. "You demolished my home? Shredded my grandmother's quilt?"

He started the engine and shifted gears, accelerating on the icy gravel road.

Asia averted her eyes, choosing to focus her anger at the mound of fast-food wrappers and soda cups scattered along the floorboard. The older vehicle's lack of shock absorption had her bouncing on the torn seat cushion. The tires slammed into a series of potholes as they rumbled over the rough terrain.

The country roads were dark, and the dim headlights provided little help in assessing where they were. Asia tried to survey the archaic interior, but the lack of light made that difficult. Based on the red leather seats that suffered from multiple punctures, the vehicle was at least twenty years old and filthy.

Her gaze traveled across to the driver. Two chrome holes indicated the place where the headrest should've been. Her captor sat low, almost casual, as if he were cruising on a hot summer night. He still wore the gorilla mask, no doubt impairing his vision.

She leaned forward, peering over his shoulder. "Where are—"

"Sit back!" He backhanded her, then glared over his shoulder.

Asia's forehead stung from the hit, fury warming her body.

The tires smashed into another hole and the car fishtailed, tossing her around in the seat. She sat crumpled, chin pressing against her chest, and an idea sprouted. Gymnastics had been a lifetime ago, but the training remained ingrained in her mind.

Ignoring the pain in her protesting shoulder, Asia spread her shoulders as wide as her restraints allowed, creating a large circle behind her back.

"What are you doing?" he growled, watching her in the rearview mirror.

She shrugged. "Just trying to stay in the seat like you said. The potholes are crazy around here."

He grunted.

Asia kept her eye on the mirror, wriggling her rear through her hooped arms. She paused, then slid her bound wrists under her legs. Another pothole allowed her to lift her knees and pull them through the opening. At last, she maneuvered her hands onto her lap.

She righted herself, took a deep breath and lunged forward, throwing her arms over the man's head and neck. With every ounce of strength, she leaned backward, using the duct tape restraints and her full body weight to choke the driver. He yelled and released the wheel, causing the car to skid on the icy road.

He grappled, fighting to regain control with one hand, clawing at her arms with the other. Her hoodie layered over the sweater protected her from injury.

She locked her feet in place on the floorboards and pulled back harder, even as the headlights of an approaching vehicle blinded her. Her captor let go of his hold on the steering wheel, focusing more on fighting for air. The car swerved into the oncoming lanes and the path of an advancing SUV.

Asia tried to grab the wheel, but her reaction time wasn't fast enough, and they collided.

An explosion of crushing metal and shattering glass reverberated inside the vehicle. The impact thrust Asia forward, slamming her nose into the back of her captor's skull.

Pain blasted over her face and stars danced before her eyes.

Then everything stilled, and only the ringing in her ears and the burning in her nose remained. Freeing her still-bound wrists from the man's neck, she shifted among the shards of window glass and groped for the door handle.

She stumbled out of the car then leaned against the rear panel, pressing her arm against her bleeding nose.

An older woman rushed toward her, arms flailing wildly. "Are you crazy? You drove—" She stopped short, her gaze bouncing between Asia's bound wrists and the gorilla-masked driver still unconscious in the crashed vehicle. She gasped, fingers pressed against her lips. "Sweet child. What happened to you?"

"Please. Help me." Asia's words came out thick over the iron taste in her mouth. "Call the police."

"Now what?" Slade climbed out of the pickup, slamming the door. Hopelessness weighed on his shoulders.

After an hour of searching the town and surrounding roads, he and Trey returned to the house, having made no progress. If Quenten's killer had abducted her, he'd… No, Slade wouldn't go there.

Ever the optimist, Trey said, "We work the clues we have, starting with identifying the men in that video."

His brother's calm demeanor should've encouraged Slade, but each passing second hammered a new nail of worry into his heart.

Why hadn't he stayed by her side? Why hadn't he clued in on her uncharacteristically reserved manner tonight? Was it time to notify Sergeant Oliver?

The conflicting questions battled in an endless circular argument. If Asia had escaped by choice, she was a fugitive. However, if someone kidnapped her, activating a legion of law enforcement officers to search for her would be beneficial. Either way, she'd be arrested and safe. Unless Zander's suspicions proved true. If there was a mole within the department, putting Asia in jail made her accessible and placed her in worse danger. Impossible decisions.

Slade followed behind Trey, each step heavier than the last. They paused on the front porch as Trey inserted the key. "That's weird."

Too tired and disheartened to focus, Slade muttered, "What?"

Trey removed his Glock and stepped to the side, lowering his voice. "Didn't you lock up before we left?"

That got Slade's attention. He withdrew his service weapon. Trey pushed open the door and Magnum bolted through the entrance, nose to the ground. Within seconds, they'd cleared the home and reconvened in the kitchen. Slade's gut said something was off, yet nothing appeared out of place.

"Maybe in our hurry—"

Slade's gaze traveled across the small space and landed on the dining table. "My laptop's gone!"

"Are you sure you didn't stash it before we took off?"

Dread clung to Slade's shoulders. He'd lost the video and failed Asia again. "No, that would've been the smart thing, which is the opposite of pretty much everything I've done today." He slumped into a chair and slammed his hand down on the table, knocking over the salt and pepper shakers. "Why didn't I grab my computer?"

"Hang on." Trey ran out of the house and returned with his laptop bag, sporting a wide grin.

"What're you smiling about?"

"Do you still have Asia's whale?"

"Yes!" He'd forgotten about the figurine in his jacket pocket. Slade quickly pulled out the whale and withdrew the hidden SD card, passing it to his brother.

Trey inserted the card into his laptop, and his fingers flew across the keys. "Make coffee. This may take a while."

Slade set the maker to Brew then paced between the living room and the kitchen. "How's it going?"

"Go lie down. Your patrolling is distracting. I'll holler as soon as I have something."

Frustrated and too tired to argue, Slade moved to the couch and flopped onto the hard cushions. He leaned back and closed his eyes. "Fine, but I just need five minutes."

The ringing of Slade's phone jerked him awake. Oliver. "Sarge."

"Asia's at the hospital."

Slade bolted upright. "What? Is she okay?"

"She escaped her kidnapper, but she's pretty shook-up with minor injuries. Doc says she'll be released within the hour."

Slade swallowed. "Thank You, Lord."

"Her captor's unconscious, and I've assigned trooper security to him. She isn't talkative, just keeps saying she wants to see you."

"I'm on my way." Slade pushed up from the couch and walked to the kitchen.

Trey sat, brows furrowed and forehead creased, staring at the computer. He glanced up at Slade's entry.

Oliver's tone grew harder. "How is it that Mrs. Stratton was abducted, and I wasn't notified?"

Slade cringed. "I promise to give you every detail, but I've got a lead. Please give me a little more time."

Trey shook his head.

"You don't ask for much, do you, Jackson?" Oliver snorted.

"Sir."

"You've got until noon. I'll meet you in the lobby."

"Thank you, sir." Slade disconnected and gave Trey a quick synopsis.

"Thank God." Trey sighed, leaning back.

"I need your truck."

"I'll go with you."

"No, we're running out of time. Have you made any progress with the video?"

Trey dug the keys from his pocket and tossed them to Slade. "Yes, but it's slow."

"Keep at it." Slade glanced at his watch and cringed. Six thirty. An hour and a half before the meeting with Jonah. "I'll call from the road."

He rushed out the door and squealed down the street, exceeding every speed limit. "Thank You, Lord."

Asia was alive, and he'd never let her out of his sight again.

The commute seemed to take forever, and when the hospital came into view, Slade had to force himself to park the vehicle and not drive through the emergency entrance. As he pulled out the keys, a text arrived from Jonah with the meeting location.

Sergeant Oliver waited in the lobby with Asia. Slade's heart stuck in his throat at her disconcerting black eye and swollen nose.

At his approach, she rushed into his arms, whispering, "I'm sorry."

Oliver's hard stare expressed concern and anger, but thankfully, he didn't demand additional information. Once Asia calmed down, Oliver informed them that her captor was a criminal known for his cartel dealings. She rambled about her escape, explaining her injuries.

For the hundredth time, Slade considered confessing about the meeting with Jonah, but one look at Asia's pleading eyes and he resisted.

After what seemed like an eternity, Slade and Asia headed out to the highway. She held an ice pack to her face where color encircled her eye. "I'm sorry for climbing out the window."

"We'll talk about all of that later. Right now, we've got to meet Jonah. We're already running behind." Slade's hands remained tight on the steering wheel.

"He called? You talked to him? When? What did he say?" Asia's rapid-fire questions prevented him from answering.

Slade gave her a quick rundown of the events, starting with Jonah's call and ending with the contact's meeting demands. "He was adamant that we come alone."

"Thank you for not telling Sergeant Oliver about Jonah or about me running away."

"I'm already on his list—no need to drag you there too."

"My emotions were so over-the-top, I spent most of the time crying," Asia admitted. "I told them the man kidnapped me from the safe house. I'm so grateful they caught him."

"From what I understand, you knocked him out."

"The car accident did that." She gave him a wry smile.

"The man's got a lengthy criminal history, and my guess is he was hired as a mercenary. I'm anxious to know who he works for. Sergeant Oliver promised to keep me updated."

"Was Trey able to lighten the video? Did you identify the other men?" Asia's averted gaze and sheepish response made her look more like a rebellious teenager caught after curfew than a kidnapping survivor.

"He's working on it. He'll meet us at the location."

She jerked to look at him. "But Jonah said to come alone! What if he sees Trey and leaves? We'll never get any information. This is my last chance before you arrest me today!"

Slade worked his jaw, hesitating. "You overheard my conversation with Oliver last night, didn't you?"

She nodded.

A fresh wave of guilt passed over him. "I should've been forthcoming with you."

"True, but it wouldn't have changed my stupid escape attempt. I was—am—afraid, and I responded out of fear."

Asia's humble and vulnerable reply had him eager to reassure her. "Fear is a liar. You're the bravest woman I've ever known." He glanced at her, sunlight accentuating her dark eyes.

Her cheeks warmed with color, and she grinned. "You would've been proud of my attack on him. He never saw it coming. Literally, thanks to the gorilla mask."

Slade smiled. "After seeing your moves on those creeps yesterday, I have no doubt it was impressive." He avoided the discussion about Trey's assistance, but Asia's stubbornness wouldn't be thwarted.

"Please. Jonah's the only chance I have left. We can't mess up this meeting."

"Trey will remain discreet. We'd be fools to walk in there without backup—"

"No! Tell him to stay away. He can't show up. Slade. Please!" Her panicked tone worried him. Two sleep-deprived nights were making her hysterical. "I know you're right, but it's too risky."

"Okay, okay. Settle down." Slade lifted his phone and dialed. "Trey, I need for you to stand down."

"Are you insane?" Trey's voice increased to near-screaming levels.

"Asia's terrified Jonah won't show and—"

She nibbled on a fingernail and turned away.

"Your safety is more important. Sergeant Oliver just dropped me off at my house. I'm picking up my patrol truck and I'll be on my way to meet you."

"Did he come alone? Did you tell him about the meeting?"

Asia grasped his arm, alarm in her dark eyes.

Trey exhaled, annoyance in his tone. "Chill. No, I didn't tell him about the meeting, but I still think it's wrong not to include him. And you're welcome."

Slade heaved a sigh of relief. "Thank you. What about the video?"

"I've got my laptop with me. I'll work on it while waiting for you. Outside the location. As we *agreed.*"

He shifted in his seat, the intensity of Asia's gaze drilling into him, demanding not to give in. "The video is the most important part. If Jonah isn't reliable or—"

"You're not doing this alone." Trey's voice hardened.

Slade frowned. "Asia's right. We need Jonah's information. Continue to work on the footage, and if you make any progress or find anything, call me."

"No—"

"Jonah's text said no phones allowed, so I'll have to leave my burner in your truck. I'll check in as soon as I can. If you don't hear from me by eight thirty, bring the cavalry."

"You can't—"

Slade rolled his eyes. "It'll be fine."

"I don't like this."

"Me either." He disconnected.

"Well?" Asia swiveled to face him.

"He's not happy."

"I gathered that by his screeching, and it's not that I disagree, but I'm against an impossible wall."

Slade nodded as foreboding hung on his shoulders. Were they walking straight to their deaths?

"Thank you."

He didn't reply.

"I don't blame you anymore. You've been a wonderful support, and I appreciate all you've done to help me. If Jonah turns out to be a dud and we don't die in this meeting, I promise not to fight or be upset with you for arresting me. You did the best you could, and I'm forever grateful."

He hadn't expected that. "As long as we're offering our confessions…" Slade frowned and worked the steering wheel.

"Let's not go there right now. Sounds too much like we're preparing to say goodbye." Asia flipped on the radio and a baritone rendition of "Blue Christmas" belted from the speakers. She glanced away. "It's Christmas Eve, and all I can think about is whether I'll spend the holidays alone in jail."

Perhaps Asia should say her goodbyes. After everything she'd endured up to this point, it seemed danger lurked around every corner, and really, how many times could one person dodge death?

Slade reached over and grabbed her hand, giving it a light squeeze. His touch was comforting and disconcerting at the same time, but she didn't resist. "I won't let you go to jail. I meant what I said last night. I care about you. And I realize my timing's horrible and it's probably wrong to tell you about my feelings. You have enough to contend with, but I need you to understand that I'm committed to helping you, whatever it takes."

She shook her head, unwilling to acknowledge his words or dare to assume he intended to escort her over the border. She couldn't, wouldn't deal with emotions right now. And this wasn't the time for romantic thoughts. If only her crazy feelings cooperated. Regardless of the current events, emotions suppressed her, demanding attention she didn't have the energy to give.

Slade's words lingered in her mind. Was he apologizing

for caring about her? Or just for his timing? Unsure if she felt rejected or relieved, Asia pasted on a smile.

The comfort of Slade's presence had become addicting, and that scared her. If she'd learned anything in her roller-coaster life with Zander, it was that when vulnerability levels were record high, it was wise to check your emotions. "If I'm incarcerated, promise me that you'll walk away."

"No way. I—"

She touched his lips, silencing him. "Please." Appalled that she'd made such a brazen move, she scooted closer to the door and folded her arms over her chest.

Slade turned down a private drive parallel to a grove of trees. The area north of Highway 20 could only be described as middle-of-nowhere Nebraska. He parked in front of a small red shack hidden among the overgrown bushes.

"Are you sure this is the place?" Asia leaned forward and surveyed the run-down cabin.

The morning sunlight and cloudless sky juxtaposed the darkened scenery and ominous landscape. There were no other vehicles, and the property appeared abandoned.

Had she made a huge mistake demanding Trey stay away? Palpable doubt and stress hovered between her and Slade, making the atmosphere suffocating.

He killed the engine then grabbed his phone. "What?" Slade fussed with the device and frustration crinkled his forehead.

"What's the matter?"

"There's no reception. Not even a single bar to send a text."

"Convenient. No wonder Jonah chose this place." She looked away. Slade would try to talk her out of this if she made eye contact. Determination and stubbornness fueled her.

Slade touched her arm, and she angled toward him. "Are you ready?"

"Yep, let's do this." She reached for the handle then stopped. "Wait. Trey's got the copied file on his computer, right? Should something happen to us…"

Slade tilted his head and the corner of his lip lifted slightly. Sunlight bounced off his five-o'clock shadow, and still, somehow, the man maintained his put-together appearance. "For the third time, yes, and let's not have any of that negative thinking."

She chuckled, exposing her horribly apparent nervousness. "I do feel better knowing Trey's got the footage. He is the more responsible brother, after all," Asia joked, hoping to lighten the mood.

"Very funny."

She sighed.

"Hey, you don't have to go in there. I can handle this alone—" He reached over and squeezed her hand.

Fear was a liar. She wouldn't surrender to it. "Nope, let's finish this."

Slade set his cell phone on the seat. "Well, the good news is, Trey can't reach me, so I won't have to listen to his endless efforts to convince me how stupid this is." He grinned.

"Right." They also would have no way to call for help, but that didn't need to be said.

"We need to contact Trey in precisely thirty minutes, so we'll have to hurry this meeting along and find cell phone reception."

"Got it."

They exited the truck simultaneously, their footsteps crunching on the packed snow. Only an eerie hush greeted them, and Asia shivered, trailing behind Slade. They climbed the two splintered steps to the cabin's square porch.

Slade rapped three times, per Jonah's text instructions. Several seconds ticked by. Doubt battled with trepidation, and once again Asia pondered whether they were making a huge mistake.

At last the sound of a latch released on the opposite side.

She took a step forward, but Slade gripped her hand tighter. "He said to count to ten, then enter."

Finally, Slade pushed open the door, and it creaked in greeting.

They entered cautiously, Slade in the lead. Their footsteps thudded against the wooden-slat floor. Asia glanced over her shoulder, unsure whether closing their only method of retreat was the safest option.

She rammed into Slade, unaware he'd stopped walking. The impact sent a fresh wave of pain up her already broken nose. Blinking away the accompanying tears, she gently touched her face and scanned the open area, void of furniture except for the round oak table where a man sat, gun aimed.

"Gilade?" Slade asked, his voice a mix of concern and confusion.

Asia peered around him, curiosity outweighing fear.

The man lowered the weapon and leaned back, legs stretched out in front of him, hands folded on his lap. Asia guessed him to be in his fifties. His shoulder-length silver hair hung in waves, framing a face that revealed a history with acne. "Trooper Jackson. Mrs. Stratton. Close the door, please. Then have a seat." He gestured at the two remaining chairs arranged in a half-moon around the table.

"You know each other?" Asia moved out from Slade's protective cover, earning a frown for her disregard of his instructions. She took the initiative and sat across from Jonah.

Slade shut the door as the stranger requested and moved to the table. "Asia Stratton, meet DEA agent Joe Gilade." He dropped onto the wooden-spindled chair, then shifted to the side, probably gaining a better—albeit incomplete—view of the entrance.

Asia tilted her head, her shoulders lowering slightly. "Mr. Gilade, we were to meet Jonah. Is he here?"

He chuckled. "Jonah's my first name, but I prefer Joe. My grandmother named me. She was big into Bible stories."

She grinned as understanding filtered through her sleep-deprived brain. "Jonah and the whale."

A twinge of confusion passed over his expression, disappearing as quickly. Apparently, he wasn't familiar with the reference.

She faced Slade. "What's your relationship with Jonah?"

"We've worked together a few times on drug task force cases," he explained, wariness tainting his tone.

Asia waited for him to continue, but he offered nothing more. Was he relieved or on guard? His terse response had her wondering…was Jonah on the right side of the law? Or had they just entered another layer of corruption?

"Did you bring the card?" Jonah got down to business.

Slade squared his shoulders. "First, clue us in to the big mystery."

Jonah shook his head and interlaced his fingers. "Less information is better for both of you. At this point, you two still have plausible deniability. It's safer that you're not dragged deeper in the mud."

Asia flattened her hands on the table and forced calmness into her voice. "I'm living knee-deep in the mud." The blank look on Jonah's face irritated her, and she tossed control out the window. "This," she said, gesturing toward her black eye and broken nose, "is the result of being hunted and almost killed several times over this card. I've more than earned an explanation."

Slade touched her hand and intervened in his placating manner. "What if I get the details and we discuss it later?"

Asia narrowed her gaze and pursed her lips. That wasn't an option.

"Fair enough." Jonah ran a hand over his salt-and-pepper goatee, revealing the fullness of his pianist-length fingers. Compassion and kindness filled his dark eyes as he addressed Asia. "What I'm about to share is top secret. If you tell anyone outside this meeting, you'll not only destroy my career, you'll place yourself in worse danger."

"I understand." Asia squared her shoulders.

Jonah sighed. "Very well. Your husband, Zander, was my CI."

"Your confidential informant?" she clarified.

"Sir, with all due respect, I'm confused. If Zander worked for you, why wasn't it cleared with the patrol?" Slade interrupted.

Exactly what Asia was wondering.

Jonah sighed again. "Sergeant Oliver sent Zander to me, hoping I could help reduce the hefty drug-trafficking charges he faced. A cop in prison…well…that's not a good thing. Zander requested to be a CI and bargained with a promise to deliver evidence against Quenten and his partners. He'd already established a relationship as an insider with them. However, the patrol wasn't apprised because Zander was certain there was a mole within the department. He needed to continue his ruse with Quenten. We couldn't chance Quenten's spy exposing Zander's cover without enough evidence to put all those involved behind bars."

Asia pressed a finger to her temple. The overwhelming information was almost too much to take in. "How long had this been going on?"

"A few months," Jonah replied in a too-calm tone, as if he were relaying the weather forecast. "Zander's claims of corruption included District Attorney Grayson Kramer and my boss, Harold Donovan."

"The head of the DEA? He's one of the guys on the video!" Slade slapped the table.

Asia startled, then grew frustrated at herself for being so jumpy.

Slade's neck reddened, and he replied sheepishly, "Sorry. I was sure I'd seen him before."

"Never heard of him." Her gaze darted between the men, unbelieving and slightly bewildered.

Jonah grunted. "Without evidence to substantiate Zander's outlandish claims, we couldn't proceed with an investigation. You can understand why I wasn't willing to just dive in. If his accusations weren't verifiable, we'd all be finding new careers, or worse, mortgaging our homes for legal fees to keep out of prison."

"If you were certain Zander had the video, why not finish this?" Slade asked.

"Zander's allegations of corruption ran far above both our pay grades. His word alone wasn't a reliable source." Jonah hesitated, as if considering whether to share more.

"I'm well aware of my husband's drug-addiction problems, if that's what you're referring to," Asia assured him.

Jonah's forehead creased. "I'm sure you endured the worst of his habit's repercussions."

Asia glanced down and swallowed the lump in her throat, grateful when he continued. "Zander guaranteed he had evidence. The night we were to meet, he disappeared and wasn't seen alive again."

A strange surge of resentment blasted through her. "Shouldn't you have protected him? I mean, if he went to all the trouble to get the video, you were responsible for keeping him safe."

Jonah's expression remained stable, but Asia caught the hint of sadness in his eyes. "Ma'am, because of Zander's history, there weren't a lot of options. He had to provide the proof first. He feared prison and Quenten's repercussions, so he demanded the terms of our agreement in writing before sharing the information."

"And that took more time," Asia concluded.

"Yes. Zander ensured he had two copies, both in safe-keeping, but refused to hand anything over without written confirmation to keep him out of prison. The papers should've been signed by District Attorney Grayson Kramer the morning Zander disappeared."

Slade pushed back from the table and paced. "Convenient."

Jonah continued, "Zander stated he had made alternative arrangements should something happen to him, but he never told me any of the details. It's our belief Quenten discovered and subsequently destroyed the recording."

Slade shifted. Was he concerned Jonah was dirty? "I want to believe you. Tell me what's on the video."

"As I've explained, I haven't seen it. I understand there's a meeting between the interested parties, and I'm hoping something that also proves the allegation about the mole."

"The scenes will require enhancements to lighten the footage. Donovan and Quenten are distinguishable. I'm unsure about the third," Slade explained.

Asia bit her lip. Slade hadn't confessed Trey was already working on a copy. Was Jonah not trustworthy?

"We've got access to some of the best computer techs in the world. If there's any way to do that, they'll figure it out." Jonah glanced at the door.

The hair on the back of her neck rose, and she looked over her shoulder. "Are you waiting for someone?"

"No, but I'm sure you're as uncomfortable with this clandestine meeting as I am," Jonah replied.

"Definitely, but I have so many questions. For instance, I'm confused. District Attorney Kramer—the same person demanding my arrest today for a murder I didn't commit—was supposed to sign Zander's agreement?"

The men exchanged a look she couldn't quite decipher.

"Yes," Slade provided.

"He's the other man in the video! The guy was dirty. No wonder he wants me arrested." Asia's stomach twisted into knots.

Jonah nodded. "If the footage is as you describe and the techs can lighten the scenes so that the parties are distinguishable, it will confirm Zander's accusations."

"I thought the mole was a trooper, but the man who kidnapped Asia is lying unconscious in the hospital after their car accident."

Asia exhaled relief that Slade didn't include the part about her running away.

Jonah leaned forward. "Have you identified him?"

"Yes, and he's got a rap sheet as long as the Mississippi River. A known criminal, not someone who works at the patrol," Slade explained.

Jonah nodded. "So we still have one more person to name. The mole is the one connection we've struggled to make. He's succeeded in staying under the radar. Without the complete puzzle, our case will unravel. We need to ensure a full conviction of all involved. Does the video implicate him?"

Slade shrugged. "Hard to say until the footage is enhanced."

"I see." Jonah ran a hand over his goatee again.

"Sir, may I ask some hard questions?" Asia asked.

"Of course."

"Who killed Zander? And who killed Quenten?"

Jonah steepled his fingers. "We believe Zander died as a result of Quenten's interrogation methods." His words were spoken carefully. "He got word about the video, I'm guessing via the mole. If my suppositions are correct, Quenten took matters into his own hands, believing he could black-mail Donovan. He thought he'd accomplished his goal until Zander slipped about making two copies."

Asia connected the dots. Zander was murdered before he released the location. She jumped up.

The action had Jonah drawing his gun, and his chair toppled backward. Slade was at her side instantly.

"Sorry, didn't mean to startle you," she said, eliciting exasperated grimaces from both men.

"Don't make sudden moves. It's dangerous," Jonah replied, adjusting his chair.

Both men sat while Asia paced. "If you knew Quenten killed Zander, why haven't you told Sergeant Oliver? And what about Quenten? I'm accused of murdering him!"

"We have proof Donovan ordered Quenten's elimination. However—"

"What proof?" Slade interjected.

"A recorded phone call between Donovan and a man. Whoever he's talking to agrees to kill Quenten, but there's nothing that points to the actual shooter. Thankfully, your amnesia created issues and gave me time to work on the recording. Well played, by the way." Jonah smirked.

"I wasn't playing," Asia snapped.

"Asia's tox screen showed scopolamine in her system," Slade explained. "However, the evidence is stacked against her. Gunshot residue and her fingerprints on the gun."

"I accidentally grabbed the gun, but I didn't knowingly shoot it," Asia blurted.

"I see. Except that with the scopolamine injection, your memory was compromised, and the gunshot residue indicates you did, in fact, shoot the gun." Jonah leaned back.

Asia slumped against the wall. This was hopeless.

"Wait." Slade flattened his hands on the table. "There

was a partial print on the gun. The killer could've forced Asia to hold the weapon, then wrapped his hands around hers and taken the shot. That would explain the partial print, and the lab would have something to test it against."

"Only if the fingerprint matches one of the implicated men," Jonah added.

"This is unreal." Asia's knees buckled, and she dropped onto the chair.

"There's a puzzling component to all of this. Quenten was hit directly in the forehead. We can't figure out why he'd just sit there," Slade said.

Jonah moved around the table. "The cartel used succinylcholine in many of their more lethal dealings. It paralyzes the victim but keeps them conscious."

"And unless it's specifically tested for, it won't show up in blood or urine samples," Slade concluded.

"Do you have the SD card?" Jonah inquired, as if the exchange had never occurred.

"This is like a spy movie, and I'm waiting for the credits to start rolling," Asia mumbled.

"I'm sorry you were caught in the middle. Once you give me that SD card, I can wrap this mess up."

"And get her exonerated?" Slade pressed.

Jonah gave her a solemn nod. "I hope so. Have your lab test for succinylcholine in Quenten's system."

"I'll do it first thing today."

Jonah could've demanded the video, but instead, he treated her with consideration. Asia withdrew the card and passed it to him. The appreciation in his expression spoke volumes as he tucked the card into his plaid shirt pocket.

"All of this nightmare for that little piece of plastic." Asia shook her head. "I still have so many questions."

"I can't attest to everything Zander may or may not have done, but aside from his drug addiction, which he had under control the last two months of his life, his actions were heroic," Jonah stated.

Why wasn't that a comfort?

"I believe you're one of the good guys, but understand that arrangements have been made for a copy of the video to go to the media should anything happen to either of us," Slade explained.

"Understood. I'll get the evidence into the hands of the DEA administrator immediately. She can clear Asia of the charges and indict the guilty parties."

"So this is over?" Asia searched both men's faces.

"No, but it's a great beginning. We still need someone in authority to acknowledge the accusations," Slade answered.

She held a hand against her throat. "I didn't believe Zander. He really was trying to make things right."

Jonah met her eyes. "Yes, ma'am. I'm not defending his actions, Mrs. Stratton, but he did confess his love for you and regrets for endangering you. His biggest concern was for your safety."

His words released the shards of anger still piercing her heart. "He did?"

Slade touched her shoulder. "Asia, I need to tell you something."

She gave him her full attention. "Zander came to me and told me he was in deep. He asked me to arrest him. He reasoned Quenten would think Zander had been caught instead of betraying him."

Asia blinked, processing the information. "But he—"

"—hoped to go into WITSEC and testify once he had enough evidence. He didn't tell me anything more than that." Slade's eyebrows furrowed. "I never should've agreed to it, but Zander was worried you'd be Quenten's next target. That's the only reason I complied."

"Zander had quite the escape plan figured out," Asia replied.

"Can you ever forgive me?" Slade asked.

She tilted her head, taking him in—this man who'd endured her anger in order to protect his friend. And her. This man who'd demonstrated how much he cared by his actions and support. "There's nothing to forgive."

"Listen, we should get moving and ensure this lands in the right hands." Jonah stood.

A snap outside jerked Asia's attention. "Did you hear that?"

"What's wrong?" Slade's eyes searched hers.

"I don't know." She pressed her fingers to her lips, while uneasiness hovered. Was she paranoid?

Jonah withdrew his gun and moved against the wall near the small window, peering out. He shook his head.

Slade glanced down at his watch. They had to leave now, or they'd miss the check-in with Trey, and he'd send in the cavalry. "We need to go."

"Agreed," Jonah said.

The door flew open, flooding the cabin with sunlight that silhouetted the intruders. The first stepped forward and Asia blinked several times, heart pounding in her throat. "No."

"What a wonderful little meeting. Sorry we're late."

ELEVEN

Kent Beardly sauntered in, followed by District Attorney Grayson Kramer and DEA director Harold Donovan. The men eclipsed the cabin entry with their three-piece suits, arrogance and guns.

"Put down your weapon, Gilade," Donovan ordered.

With a venomous glare, Gilade placed his Glock on the table and stepped away.

Panic swarmed Slade, and dread filled his heart.

They were trapped. He jerked to look at Asia, desperate to protect her, halted only by the three guns pointed in their direction. He needed to get closer to her. "Nice Sig Sauer, Beardly. Thanks for having the decency not to use your department-issued weapon." Slade took a step closer to Asia.

"My Glock's too traceable. You figured that out, didn't you, Mrs. Stratton?" Beardly laughed. "Move another inch and I'll be forced to show off the Sig."

Slade gritted his teeth. They'd lingered too long in the cabin. Why hadn't he forced them to leave? Why had he brought Asia?

Kramer took three lengthy strides and closed the distance between them. "So, you're Zander's *killer* widow." He laughed.

Asia glowered at him but didn't respond.

"And you're the two-faced district attorney spouting your zero-tolerance policy," Slade countered.

"You should've arrested her as you were instructed." Kramer shrugged.

"Are you all in this together?" Gilade hissed. "You played me?" He glanced between Slade and Asia.

"No way," Slade replied, strangely reassured at Gilade's distress. The man wasn't dirty.

"Rule-follower Jackson? Never." Beardly cackled. "You know one of the best things about you, Trooper? You're so predictable and such a devoted big brother. Your sibling's just not quite as smart, though, is he?"

"If you hurt Trey—" Slade stepped toward Beardly, fists clenched.

"Careful, Trooper." Donovan aimed his gun at Asia.

Slade froze, constraining the surge of adrenaline and anger.

"How did you find us?" Asia asked.

"Don't short out your simple brain," Beardly said. "We have brilliant minds at the patrol, and nothing is impossible."

Oh, please, Lord, bring help.

Had Beardly gone after Trey? Slade's heart ached at the possibility. No. His brother was savvy and smart. Beardly was using the manipulation technique to throw off his confidence, to get inside his head. The man didn't know about the check-in time, and when Slade failed to contact Trey, he'd call for backup as planned. All Slade had to do was stall. Hope like a single candle in a hurricane illuminated inside him. Whatever happened, Trey had everything he needed to take down these monsters.

As long as his brother and Asia survived, nothing else mattered.

Asia gasped, and she pointed at Beardly, eyes wide. "It was you!"

"Shut your mouth, Mrs. Stratton," Beardly growled.

"No, I remember now. You were there that night."

The room grew silent, everyone watching Asia, waiting for her to speak. "You knocked on my apartment door, just before I was going to go to bed. I peered through the peephole and saw you!" She pointed at Beardly again.

"It's too bad you didn't recall that sooner," Beardly taunted. "Think how it would've helped you. Now it's too late."

Asia continued, "I recognized you from the funeral, so I let you in." She clamped a hand over her mouth.

Slade shifted toward her, but Kramer shook his head, gun trained on him.

"You were so enraged, screaming at me about a video," she whispered.

"What else can you remember?" Slade pressed.

"It doesn't matter!" Beardly's guttural roar sent a shiver up Slade's spine. He shoved Asia into a chair and crossed the room, back to them. "Your memories are irrelevant." His immediate shift into a controlled persona was creepier than his previous temper tantrum.

The investigator's mannerisms resembled a toddler and seemed to suck Donovan and Kramer into the drama. The distraction allowed Slade to discreetly gesture for Asia to get down. She nodded and shifted closer to the wall.

Beardly faced Slade. "You're used to having blood on your hands, though, aren't you? Having lived with Zander's all this time."

Asia screamed, distracting Beardly.

Slade took the opportunity and lunged, driving a punch to the smug investigator's jaw. Beardly countered with an awkward roundhouse that slid off Slade's arm and sent fresh anger surging through him. He lowered his shoulder and ran into Beardly's midsection, tackling him. Beardly lost hold of the Sig, and it skidded across the cabin floor.

In his peripheral, Slade saw Jonah attack Donovan. The momentary disruption gave Beardly an opening, and he delivered a blow to Slade's kidney, radiating pain in his lower back and catching him off guard. Adrenaline coursed through his veins and Slade connected with a right hook, jolting Beardly's face to the side. Fury emboldened him, and he drilled one final jab to the backstabber's nose.

A gunshot rang out above Slade's head, stilling the brawl. He immediately jerked to see if Asia was okay. Her face had gone ashen, and Kramer gripped her injured arm.

"That's enough," Kramer said, amusement in his expression. "Feel better, Jackson? Gilade?" Then to Beardly, "Invest in some defensive-tactics training. He would've knocked you out." He laughed, pushing Asia, and she dropped beside Slade.

Beardly's face turned bright red as he stood, then stepped backward, distancing himself from Slade. Donovan kicked Jonah, who was sprawled out on his back.

Slade pushed himself up, refusing to acknowledge the pain in his body.

"Give me the card." Donovan yanked Asia up by her injured arm, evoking a yelp.

"Let go of her," Slade warned, ready to take on the traitor DEA agent.

Donovan rested the tip of his Sig Sauer against Asia's temple. "Spare me your tough-guy talk."

"What are you doing, Donovan?" Gilade stepped forward but was stopped by Donovan's glare and Kramer's trained weapon. "You're above this."

"No one's above anything, Gilade. Aren't you sick of working endless hours and watching three criminals emerge for each one you arrest? You can't win. But you can make a lot of money with a little ingenuity." Everything about Donovan said the man didn't have a bone of integrity.

"What about justice?"

Slade watched Gilade's body language. Was he buying time? Was Gilade privy to something that could help them? Whatever his reasoning, Slade appreciated the delay.

"Justice is a fantasy." Donovan gripped Asia's hair in his hand and tugged her toward him. "Now, tell me where the video is."

"She doesn't have it!" Slade hollered, reaching for Donovan.

Kramer sent a bullet next to Slade's boots. "Move another inch and I'll take out your leg."

Slade backed up, his mind racing for a way to end this standoff.

Asia shook her head and, to her credit, didn't look at Gilade. "I don't have it."

"Don't play games with me! Your worthless husband gave you the card, and my incompetent, brainless cohorts—" Kramer glared at Beardly "—failed to retrieve it. My patience is worn paper-thin. One more chance," he warned.

"I don't have it," Asia repeated.

"Tell you what." Kramer lifted his Sig Sauer and pressed it against her arm. "Someone better hand me that card or I'll shoot each of you several times until I get my answers, starting with her."

"No! I'll hand the card over to you, if you let Asia go," Slade bargained.

"Slade, no," she argued.

"It's over." Slade prayed she understood.

Kramer lowered his gun. "Smart."

"Get Asia out of here first." Slade sent her a look, hoping she'd comply. *Be quiet. Leave and get help.*

"Card first. Then she can leave," Donovan contended. "Nonnegotiable."

"In Gilade's shirt pocket." Slade met the agent's disparaging expression and flattened lips.

Gilade's face went from disbelief to anger. "Nice, Jackson."

Donovan stormed to his agent and ripped out the SD card, then pocketed it before shoving Gilade. He stumbled backward and, using the force, reached for his gun lying on the table. He aimed, and Donovan shot a round into Gilade's shoulder, knocking him to the ground. He turned and pointed the barrel at Slade.

Asia screamed and fought against Kramer's hold. "Be still, sweetheart, or you're next."

Slade launched at Kramer as a bullet whizzed past his ear, grazing the tip. Slade drove a fist into his gut. He released his hold on Asia and she bolted toward the door, but Beardly got there first.

"I wouldn't do that again," Donovan said from behind. The cold steel of his gun pressed against Slade's back.

Gilade groaned, holding his shoulder. Slade stood frozen, chest heaving with exertion and fury.

Donovan shoved Slade into a chair. "That's a good boy. Now sit down and shut up." He addressed Beardly. "Go outside and finish setting up everything."

Asia moved out of his way as Beardly scurried out the door.

"Okay, princess, tie them up," Kramer ordered Asia, tossing her plastic zip ties.

Her eyes widened. "But you said—"

"I said I'd let *you* go. Of course, you'll never really be free, will you? What with all that evidence against you." Kramer's sardonic laugh filled the room. He withdrew a small black box from his pocket and displayed it for them.

"Make any sudden moves, gentlemen, and we'll all go up in flames."

Slade's stomach knotted. A detonator.

Asia moved in slow, dragging steps until she reached Gilade. He winced as she bound his wrists behind him. "I'm so sorry."

"None of this is on you," he grunted. Crimson stained his white-and-black-plaid shirt. The man would bleed to death if they didn't get out of here.

She knelt before Slade, binding his ankles to the chair's base. Each reluctant move broke his heart a little more. She glanced up, meeting his gaze, and the realization slammed into him with the force of a rodeo bull.

He didn't just care about her. He was in love with Asia.

Once again, Slade's timing was terrible, but he refused to deny it—if only to himself—any longer. He opened his mouth to speak, then clamped it shut. Telling her now wouldn't help. She had to leave this place, and he would die at Beardly's corrupt hands.

Kramer yanked her to her feet. "Let's go!"

Donovan led the trio out of the cabin. Asia glanced over her shoulder, fear and desperation etched in her worried expression. Would Kramer and Donovan keep their word? Would she be okay?

The door slammed shut.

Slade struggled to breathe against the tsunami of panic rising in his chest. "Please, Lord, help Asia. She needs You now."

"Pray for *us*! They're going to blow up the cabin!" Gilade screeched.

Slade jerked against his restraints. He hadn't even realized he'd spoken the prayer aloud.

He heard raised voices outside.

A series of gunshots permeated the air, followed by a woman's scream.

"Asia!" Slade tried to jump up but succeeded only in thrusting himself forward. He landed face-first on the wooden floor. The shock of the impact radiated through his nose.

The bindings dug into his skin, but the face flop broke his ankles free from the zip ties. He rolled to the side and, in an awkward caterpillar maneuver, stood with the chair still attached like a turtle shell. Slade ran backward, prepared for impact.

An explosion rocked the cabin. Fire swarmed the room as Slade hit the wall with an *oomph*, splintering the chair. He yanked his wrists apart, breaking the restraints. His ears rang, and the room disintegrated in smoke and heat.

Slade stumbled to his feet and moved to where Gilade lay unconscious under a pile of debris. He hefted Gilade over his shoulder, then burst from the cabin, praying freedom and safety lay beyond the smoke.

Outside the inferno, Slade dropped to his knees, pain radiating up his side as he set down Gilade. He pushed up, wavering on shaky legs, and rested his hands on his knees.

Gilade grabbed his leg, startling him, and mouthed something, but Slade couldn't hear him over the pronounced ringing in his ears.

Slade turned as a man jogged toward them, his features obscured by the sunlight. He blinked. Trey? Was he hallucinating?

"Nice James Bond move!" Trey hollered.

"You're alive!" Slade embraced his brother in a bear hug. "What about Asia?"

"She's fine." Trey cut off Gilade's restraints and helped him stand.

Slade and Trey worked together assisting Gilade in walking.

They took a wide berth around the burning cabin.

"How did you get here so fast?" Slade took in the chaotic scene.

Gilade grinned. "Perfect timing!"

"I finished enhancing the video soon after we hung up and wham! That's when I saw it!" Trey's gestures grew more animated with each word. "Beardly's reflection in the window beside Quenten. At that point, Kramer and Donovan were distinguishable. I immediately called Oliver, he ordered backup and we raced here. I tried to call you—"

Gilade winced. "Sorry, my bad. I shouldn't have demanded you leave your phone. Not the smartest thinking on my part."

Slade shook his head. "Irrelevant. We had no reception."

"How did Beardly find our location?" Gilade asked.

Trey frowned. "Donovan's tech accessed your call log and saw the message."

Gilade worked his jaw. "Unbelievable."

Garnet lights strobed against the dark evergreens, giving the atmosphere a holiday ambience—except for the plethora of law enforcement and fire department vehicles surrounding the property. Firefighters tamed the flames while Oliver shouted orders, Asia by his side.

Streaks trailed from her eyes where tears had mixed with dirt and soot. She spotted Slade and sprinted to him, throwing her arms around his neck. "Thank God!"

Slade wrapped her in an embrace. To his delight, Asia melted against him. He didn't want to spend a single second away from her. Ever. "I thought you were...that they'd..." His throat tightened with emotion.

She leaned back and met his gaze. "When we walked out, troopers were waiting."

He pressed her close again, ignoring the pain and relishing the embrace.

"But the gunshots—" Gilade interjected.

Slade had almost forgotten the man was there.

"Donovan threatened to shoot me, and the troopers fired. That's when Kramer hit the detonator."

"Donovan took a hit to the knee." Trey pointed to a parked ambulance. "He'll live."

Slade turned and suppressed a grin. Donovan lay restrained and strapped to the stretcher, screaming obscenities at everyone around him.

"Where's Kramer?" He scanned the property, spotting the man kneeling in the snow, hands cuffed behind him.

"Let's get your shoulder taken care of." Trey led Gilade to the closest ambulance, giving Slade and Asia privacy.

Asia's dark eyes enveloped him, and Slade struggled to speak.

She ducked her head into his chest. "Thank you, for everything."

Adrenaline still rushing, Slade rallied his courage and said, "You amaze me. You've been through so much and—"

Someone cleared his throat. "Bro."

Slade turned. Trey. Proof his brother also bore the worst-timing-ever gene that was apparently ingrained in Jackson men.

"Oliver wants to see you," Trey said.

Slade reluctantly retreated from Asia's touch. "Stay with Trey." He walked over to where Kramer and Oliver stood.

"Confession time. Since no one's above the law, according to your zero-tolerance policy." Slade yanked the SD card from the DA's shirt pocket, ripping the fabric.

Kramer looked up, squinting against the sunlight. "Spare me."

"Okay, maybe your partner will have more to say. Whoever speaks up first has the best chance of reducing their sentence." Slade paused, allowing his words to sink in.

"Doesn't matter, Jackson," Oliver said.

"This isn't finished until he admits Asia didn't kill Quenten."

"Your girlfriend's the least of my worries," Kramer barked. "Besides, why would I help anyone but myself?"

"Because you're looking at a lifetime in prison. Speak up, starting with the truth. Who murdered Quenten?" Slade probed.

Kramer laughed. "Save your breath, Trooper."

Slade's frustration rose to new levels. He glanced to where Donovan sat hollering. "You're right. Let's see what your cronies or Donovan have to say instead." He stepped forward.

"Wait," Kramer called. "Cut me a deal. Then I'll talk."

Asia closed the distance between them and moved to Kramer's side.

Trey shrugged and mouthed "I tried."

Slade gave a jerk of his head. She wasn't easy to corral, especially when she was determined. "He won't talk to you," he warned.

She ignored him and knelt beside Kramer. "I can't speak to Zander's choices." Asia's voice was soft. "You don't owe me anything, but I'm asking you to tell me the truth about Quenten."

Kramer shook his head, adjusting his arms. "Get me a lawyer or make me a deal."

Slade stormed away, needing distance before he punched the hypocritical DA. He walked to the ambulance where Gilade sat with a female paramedic dressing his bullet wound.

"Sorry for what I said earlier," Gilade said.

Slade took a second to recall what the agent referred to. "Just stress talking."

"I thought you'd double-crossed me."

"In this crazy turn of events, that's not unreasonable to assume, but I only wanted to help Asia. If I died, at least she'd have the evidence to clear her name."

Asia and Kramer exchanged words—not heated—while Oliver hovered, holding his cell phone near Kramer's head. Was he recording? Did Kramer realize Oliver was there? After a few moments, Asia said something to Oliver, then walked toward Slade, wearing a smile that emphasized her beauty.

He met her halfway. "What was that about?"

"Kramer confessed Beardly shot Quenten just as you described, with his hands wrapped around mine."

"You got him to confess?"

"I suggested he tell the truth," Asia said, a twinkle in her eye. "And Sergeant Oliver recorded it."

She'd done more than that, but whatever worked.

Slade pulled her into his arms, catching a glimpse of Oliver over his shoulder. His supervisor gave a knowing nod and grinned, then tugged Kramer to his feet.

"Thank you," Asia whispered, inching closer. Her lips were so close he could feel the warmth of her breath. The sunlight brought out flecks of green in her chocolate-brown eyes.

He swallowed. "For what?"

"For not giving up on me."

Slade hugged her, absorbing her touch that consumed his heart and affirmed his resolve to never let Asia go. Before he talked himself out of it again, he said, "I'm sure romantic feelings are the furthest thing from your mind. It's just…we've dodged death too many times together in the past two days, and I wouldn't want anything to happen."

His throat tightened around the desert in his mouth. "Um, without you knowing. That I love you."

Asia searched Slade's eyes. Had she heard him correctly? The surrounding chaos was loud; perhaps she'd misunderstood. His confession didn't feel misplaced. Rather, his words were the period at the end of a sentence she'd longed to finish. How was that possible?

Her thoughts faded as he placed a finger under her chin and tilted her head up. She sucked in air as he leaned in.

They hovered so close, exhaling steam into the cold air. Slade brushed his lips against hers. Their connection zinged, awakening her heart and electrifying her senses from eyelashes to toenails. The shattered barriers forced Asia to face what she'd denied far too long. She met his kiss, enjoying the deliciousness.

Too soon, they separated, breathless. "Asia Stratton, you're a brave woman."

She smiled. "Love has a way of making you brave."

Slade's mouth dropped open. "Wait. Did you…? When did you…?"

Asia chuckled. "I think it happened while I was stuffed in my kidnapper's trunk. I realized I had isolated myself by justifying that it was safer being alone than hurting again. I'd blamed you, God, anybody who'd take my hits for my misery. When I released my anger, a peace I've never known before opened my heart. And there you were."

He pulled her into a hug, embracing her in the strength and tenderness of his arms. "We must discuss a few things. Like a future."

Asia's heart thudded with excitement against her rib cage. "Absolutely." She studied him, the firmness of his jaw and the smile lines around his eyes, drinking Slade in, every inch of his handsome, dirt-stained face. Before she could reason herself out of the moment, Asia initiated a kiss, gentle at first then deepening as Slade pressed her closer. The sweetness of his lips combined with tears— whether hers or his, she wasn't sure—tasted amazing, and she thanked God for giving them a second chance.

The morning stretched into evening, and at last, Slade and Asia escaped the craziness of reports, confessions and charges. They sat in the Meadow Hills bakery, at Asia's behest, for dinner and a redo on the cinnamon rolls.

Instrumental carols played on the speakers above, and lights decorating the store's windows softly faded from one color to the next.

Asia swiped a dollop of cream-cheese frosting from the corner of Slade's lip. "You're making a mess."

The anticipation of Christmas hung in the atmosphere, and for the first time in years, Asia welcomed the holiday, ready to share the wonder of Christ's birth with Slade. Their adventure had been an eye-opening experience in so many ways, and she indulged in her new freedom with an appreciation for relationships and the closeness of family.

She soaked in the shop's ambience, then gazed at Slade's handsome, clean-shaven face. He was gorgeous, dressed meticulously in a starched white cotton shirt. When had she fallen head over heels for him?

"Cinnamon rolls were your idea," he said in defense.

She shrugged. "We had to celebrate my exoneration."

"Technically, you were never charged," Slade teased. "I was impressed that Beardly confessed to whacking you on the head, shooting you when he caught you texting me and setting the timed ignition device at the safe house. The creep sang like the chicken he is."

"Chickens don't sing." She laughed.

Slade's cheeks reddened. "Ugh, I'm picking up Sergeant Oliver's annoying habit of confusing clichés."

Asia chuckled. "It's adorable."

"You have a beautiful laugh." He swiped a stray hair from her face. "Oh, and Trey insisted you travel to Iowa with us tomorrow to celebrate Christmas with the Jackson clan."

The idea of being with a real family for the holidays both terrified and excited her. "First, you'd best clear that with your folks."

"Done. Pops said they'd be hurt if you refused."

Asia's eyes filled and she blinked away the moisture. "I wouldn't dream of missing out, then."

"Outstanding!" Slade's grin was so wide it brought out the dimple she'd forgotten he had.

She touched his cheek, savoring every second with him. "Have I said thank you?"

"You have." He kissed her hand.

"With Donovan, Beardly and Kramer arrested and charged for all their crimes, and their full confession about Quenten's murder, I'm free in a way I never thought possible. And what better way to celebrate than enjoying cinnamon rolls again?" She forked a large piece of the dessert.

"I like your low expectations of celebrations. I live on a trooper's salary."

She winked. "Good thing for you, I'm accustomed to thriving on a budget. However, I should have Zander's pension and life-insurance benefits soon, and I can pay off all my debt."

"Zander came through," Slade commented.

"He did." A peace replaced the hurt that had once reigned in her heart when she discussed Zander. She took another bite then and, eager to change topics, said, "I'm excited to find a new apartment."

"Just make sure it has a very short-term lease."

Butterflies danced in her stomach.

"Do your plans also include a wonderful future with a certain Nebraska state trooper?" Slade pulled her closer, his breath warm against her cheek.

She sighed in contentment. "Definitely."

"Good." Slade leaned in, his lips parting slightly.

"Merry Christmas!" Trey exclaimed, bursting through the door with Sergeant Oliver and Joe Gilade.

Asia giggled and sat back, ears warm. She busied herself cutting another piece of dessert.

"Worst timing ever," Slade mumbled. "Christmas is tomorrow, bro."

Trey laughed, and the group dragged over chairs, joining them. "Asia invited us."

She shrugged, grinning, and stuffed a bite of cinnamon roll into her mouth.

Sergeant Oliver seemed to be the only one who understood they'd interrupted a moment. "Why don't we place our orders," he suggested, ushering Jonah and Trey to the counter.

"As I was saying…" Slade scooted closer and lifted her chin, claiming Asia's lips with a wordless promise for their future.

And her outlook had never looked brighter.

EPILOGUE

Three months later...

Asia grinned, absorbing the beauty of the spring day and taking in the landscape of rolling hills surrounding the lake. Slade parked beneath the trees coming to life with new green leaves. The scenery was brilliant against the cerulean sky adorned in marshmallow clouds.

A wooden sign near the entrance read Misty Lake Park.

She tugged her favorite fuzzy sweater tighter, excited to venture into the park. The temperatures were chilly, but fresh grass had sprouted after the long winter, and she was eager to enjoy the outdoors again.

Asia glanced at the cement path that wound among the assortment of blooming foliage. Squirrels chattered, running between trees, and the sunlight shimmered off the lake, mirroring images.

Slade turned off the engine, then faced her with a boyish grin on his handsome face. "We're here."

"This is beautiful." She exhaled. "Who knew a spring day in Nebraska could be this gorgeous?"

"This is by far one of my favorite places."

She narrowed her gaze. "Really? Then why haven't we ever been here before?"

"I was saving it for something special." His caramel eyes twinkled with conspiracy. Slade helped her from the vehicle, then hefted out the basket from the back seat. "Is it too cold for a picnic?"

"Are you kidding? We've got sunshine and fabulous weather, and it's cool enough there aren't bugs," she said with a wink.

"I love your rationalizations."

She pivoted slowly, taking in the entirety of the place, awed by the beauty all around her.

"Are you planning on standing there all day?"

"I'm enjoying the view."

"If I pass out from hunger, you'll have to carry me." Slade handed her a blanket.

"We can't have that." She tucked her arm in the crook of his, and they strolled through the picturesque park.

"What a neat idea," Asia remarked, leaning over a short wooden post and reading the plaque displaying the type of tree. "This one is a dwarf Autumn Blaze maple."

"The park specializes in tree preservation. It's actually very educational."

"Once you retire from the patrol, you can work for the Nebraska Game and Parks Commission as a tour guide." She laughed.

"At least I'd still have a uniform. I hate picking out clothes." He chuckled.

"I love a man in uniform." Asia planted a kiss on his cheek.

They walked nearer to the lake, alive with ducks quacking in an intense discussion. A man jogged by with a black Labrador at his side.

Slade grew unusually quiet, but they were comfortable with one another. Every moment no longer needed conversation.

He led her to a grassy area where tall cottonwoods with trunks bigger than both of them hovered above, providing a canopy in lavish shades of green.

"Does this work?" he asked, setting down the basket.

"Looks good to me."

He spread out the blanket. "Sure it's not too cool for you?"

"Not at all." Asia laid out their meal of fried chicken, biscuits and coleslaw. "Everything is perfect."

She sat beside Slade as he layered her plate with food. "Why are you so quiet today?"

"Just taking everything in." He leaned in, kissing her full on the lips. "But I agree, this is wonderful."

"It's probably more beautiful in the summer," Asia said, before biting into a piece of chicken.

"The Fourth of July is the best. They have a huge celebration here."

"Really? I'd love to see that."

"Done." He grinned. "Although, I must admit, I like winter."

"You do? I didn't think anybody over the age of ten liked winter," she teased.

"I don't prefer driving in whiteout conditions, but I love when snow blankets the ground. It's like God's way of providing nature a big do-over."

"I've never thought about it that way." Asia considered his words. "A do-over in life would be nice. There's so much I would've done differently." She glanced down, feeling the weight of his eyes on her.

"I wouldn't redo anything."

Asia looked up. "Really? Nothing?"

Slade tilted his head, chicken leg in hand. "Well…maybe a few things. But I've learned a lot of lessons from my mistakes. I'm not sure they'd have as solid an impact if they'd come easily. I know it's made me appreciate the gifts in my life so much more. I can honestly say many of my hardships have bloomed into blessings."

"I forgot how philosophical you get," Asia teased, wanting to change the subject.

Would she ever appreciate the adversities she endured and call them blessings? Zander had tried to correct his mistakes and died in his efforts. Still, his valiant attempt and the truth about his intentions had freed her heart, and ultimately saved her life.

They ate their fill, chatting about nothing in particular while sharing portions with a curious and brave squirrel. The day couldn't have been more perfect, and Asia was a little sad to see it end.

They worked together packing their leftovers and cleaning up their picnic.

"You know what? Leave it for now," Slade said. "Let's go for a walk."

"But shouldn't we—" She gestured toward the basket.

"It'll be fine. I don't think the squirrels are strong enough to carry it up to their tree."

Asia laughed and took his hand, the gesture so natural and comfortable.

They strolled through the park to an iron bridge. Below, a stream led from the lake to a smaller pond on the other side. They paused to watch turtles poke their heads out of the shallow water.

Slade slid his arm around her waist, turning her toward him and tipping her chin. "I love you."

"I love you too." Heat rushed up her cheeks. Her stomach flip-flopped like it did every time Slade looked at her the way he was now.

His eyes darkened, soaking her in as if he could read

right into her soul. "You've had my heart since kindergarten."

"Can a kindergartner really be in love?" she quipped, suddenly nervous.

He shrugged. "I was. You had the cutest pigtails."

"I remember you pulling them."

"I wasn't as suave back then. I've improved my moves and discovered a few things over the years." He brushed her lips softly, and warmth swirled inside her again.

"Oh yeah, what's something you've learned?"

"I let you go once, but I'll never do that again. I'd fight an army for you." He slid a stray hair away from her cheek.

"You've more than proven you're battle worthy."

"Asia." He reached into his pocket and produced a small black box.

She sucked in a breath.

Slade opened the box and revealed an antique diamond solitaire. "This was my grandmother's ring. My dad saved it for me and said I'd know when the right one came along." He withdrew the ring and held it between his thumb and forefinger. "Asia, would you do me the honor of becoming my wife?"

She studied him, and her throat tightened. *Speak.* Silent seconds ticked by. She was taking too long. He'd think she was going to say no.

Doubt shadowed Slade's face, and he glanced down. "Um...maybe this—"

Finally, Asia raised herself onto her tippy toes and wrapped her arms around his neck. The scent of his aftershave floated to her, filling her senses. "Slade Jackson, I'd love nothing more than to be your wife."

He exhaled loudly, pressing his hand against his chest. "Did you pause for effect?"

"Suspense heightens the moment," she said with a shrug.

Slade laughed. "Somehow I have a feeling life with you will never be boring."

"I promise a lifetime of adventure." Asia claimed his lips and released her heart into his capable hands.

* * * * *

If you enjoyed this story,
look for
Secret Past
by Sharee Stover.

Dear Reader,

I hope you've enjoyed Asia and Slade's adventures in *Silent Night Suspect*.

These characters are especially dear to me because they've carried such heavy burdens for so long. Asia's perceptions have tainted the way she sees everyone, even God. Slade realizes extending a tiny olive branch leads to his own healing.

If you're carrying a heavy burden or feeling like the storm is never going to pass, I hope you find encouragement in Asia and Slade's story. Rest assured, you're never alone in the Lord and good can come from even the worst circumstances.

I love hearing from readers, so please find me on my webpage at www.shareestover.com, or email me at authorshareestover@gmail.com.

May the source of all our hope bless you,
Sharee Stover

WE HOPE YOU ENJOYED THIS BOOK!

Love Inspired® SUSPENSE

Uncover the truth in these thrilling stories of faith in the face of crime from Love Inspired Suspense. Discover six new books available every month, wherever books are sold!

LoveInspired.com

LISHALO2019

AVAILABLE THIS MONTH FROM
Love Inspired® Suspense

TRUE BLUE K-9 UNIT CHRISTMAS
True Blue K-9 Unit • by Laura Scott and Maggie K. Black

The holidays bring danger and love in these two brand-new novellas, where a K-9 officer teams up with a paramedic to find her ex's killer before she and her daughter become the next victims, and an officer and his furry partner protect a tech whiz someone wants silenced.

AMISH CHRISTMAS HIDEAWAY
by Lenora Worth

Afraid for her life after witnessing a double homicide, Alisha Braxton calls the one person she knows can help her—private investigator Nathan Craig. Now hiding in Amish country, can they stay one step ahead of a murderer who's determined she won't survive Christmas?

HOLIDAY HOMECOMING SECRETS
by Lynette Eason

After their friend is killed, detective Jade Hollis and former soldier Bryce Kingsley join forces to solve the case. But searching for answers proves deadly—and Jade's hiding a secret. Can he live long enough to give Bryce a chance to be a father to the daughter he never knew existed?

CHRISTMAS WITNESS PURSUIT
by Lisa Harris

When an ambush leaves two FBI agents dead and her memory wiped, the only person witness Tory Faraday trusts is the sheriff's deputy who saved her. But even hiding on Griffin O'Callaghan's family ranch isn't quite safe enough after a dangerous criminal escapes from custody with one goal: finding her.

SILENT NIGHT SUSPECT
by Sharee Stover

Framed for the murder of a cartel boss, Asia Stratton must clear her name... before she ends up dead or in jail. State trooper Slade Jackson's convinced the crime is tied to the police corruption Asia's late husband—and his former partner—suspected. But can they prove it?

FATAL FLASHBACK
by Kellie VanHorn

Attacked and left for dead, all Ashley Thompson remembers is her name. But after park ranger Logan Everett rescues her, she discovers she's an undercover FBI agent searching for a mole in the rangers. Without blowing her cover, can she convince Logan to help her expose the traitor...before the investigation turns fatal?

LOOK FOR THESE AND OTHER LOVE INSPIRED BOOKS WHEREVER BOOKS ARE SOLD, INCLUDING MOST BOOKSTORES, SUPERMARKETS, DISCOUNT STORES AND DRUGSTORES.

LISATMBPA1219

COMING NEXT MONTH FROM
Love Inspired® Suspense

Available January 7, 2020

TRAINED TO DEFEND
K-9 Mountain Guardians • by Christy Barritt
Falsely accused of killing her boss, Sarah Peterson has no choice but to rely on her ex-fiancé, former detective Colton Hawk, and her boss's loyal husky for protection. But can they clear her name before the real murderer manages to silence her for good?

AMISH COUNTRY KIDNAPPING
by Mary Alford
For Amish widow Rachel Albrecht, waking up to a man trying to kidnap her is terrifying—but not as much as discovering he's already taken her teenaged sister. But when her first love, *Englischer* deputy Noah Warren, rescues her, can they manage to keep her and her sister alive?

SECRET MOUNTAIN HIDEOUT
by Terri Reed
A witness to murder, Ashley Willis hopes her fake identity will keep her hidden in a remote mountain town—until she's tracked down by the killer. Now she has two options: flee again...or allow Deputy Sheriff Chase Fredrick to guard her.

LONE SURVIVOR
by Jill Elizabeth Nelson
Determined to connect with her last living family member, Karissa Landon tracks down her cousin—and finds the woman dead and her son a target. Now going on the run with her cousin's baby boy and firefighter Hunter Raines may be the only way to survive.

DANGER IN THE DEEP
by Karen Kirst
Aquarium employee Olivia Smith doesn't know why someone wants her dead—but her deceased husband's friend, Brady Johnson, knows a secret that could explain it. Brady vowed he'd tell no one his friend had been on the run from the mob. But could telling Olivia save her life?

COLORADO MANHUNT
by Lisa Phillips and Jenna Night
The hunt for fugitives turns deadly in these two thrilling novellas, where a US marshal must keep a witness safe after the brother she testified against escapes prison, and a bounty hunter discovers she and the vicious gang after her bail jumper tracked the man's twin instead.

LOOK FOR THESE AND OTHER LOVE INSPIRED BOOKS WHEREVER BOOKS ARE SOLD, INCLUDING MOST BOOKSTORES, SUPERMARKETS, DISCOUNT STORES AND DRUGSTORES.

LISCNM1219